NOT NEGOTIABLE

By the Same Author

DRINK TO YESTERDAY
PRAY SILENCE
THEY TELL NO TALES
WITHOUT LAWFUL AUTHORITY
GREEN HAZARD
THE FIFTH MAN
A BROTHER FOR HUGH
LET THE TIGER DIE
AMONG THOSE ABSENT

NOT NEGOTIABLE

by

Manning Coles

✳

London

HODDER & STOUGHTON

First Printed April 1949

MADE AND PRINTED IN GREAT BRITAIN FOR
HODDER AND STOUGHTON LIMITED LONDON
BY RICHARD CLAY AND COMPANY, LTD.,
BUNGAY, SUFFOLK.

CONTENTS

I.	PROLOGUE	*p.* 9
II.	THE MAN WHO WAS AFRAID . .	*p.* 21
III.	PAPA	*p.* 35
IV.	PLEASE, ST. JOSEPH . . .	*p.* 49
V.	STEWPAN	*p.* 63
VI.	HANDCUFFS FOR HAMBLEDON . .	*p.* 77
VII.	THE BAKER'S BOY	*p.* 90
VIII.	SLUSH	*p.* 105
IX.	UNSUCCESSFUL EXPERIMENT . . .	*p.* 119
X.	BURENNE	*p.* 132
XI.	THE ROAD TO PARIS	*p.* 148
XII.	CARNATIONS FOR COLETTE . . .	*p.* 161
XIII.	"WHOSE GRAVES ARE SET" . .	*p.* 177
XIV.	LEONIE	*p.* 192
XV.	SOLDIER OF THE LEGION . . .	*p.* 202
XVI.	THE CALENDAR	*p.* 215

Grateful acknowledgements are due and offered to M. Rowet of 75 Boulevard Adolphe Max, Brussels, for the courtesy with which his close knowledge of the geography, habits and customs of Brussels was put at the author's disposal.

I

PROLOGUE

IN the days of the Second World War there was a concentration camp at Sachsenhausen. There still is, for that matter. Here were assembled, by order of the late Heinrich Himmler, a number of highly skilled engravers, printers and paper-makers, some of them men who had worked legally upon the making of currency notes in the Mints of their own countries in the years before Germany took them over. These men were well treated—if they did as they were told—handsomely fed and provided with all that they needed of raw materials, tools and machinery. Their task was to produce forged currency and they did it, to the tune of millions of whatever it happened to be. British five-pound notes were a popular brand; so were American dollar bills.

The "fivers" were originally produced as part of a scheme for depreciating British currency. Someone who knew a little about life in Britain said that £5 notes were not very common in that country, therefore ordinary people were not very familiar with their appearance, therefore any small faults which appear in even the best forgeries were not likely to be readily noticed. Let five-pound notes be scattered, singly but in large numbers, over the country from the air. People would naturally pick them up and spend them, several hundred thousand spurious notes would enter the currency and with any luck the amount of trouble caused would be rewarding. So immense numbers of these notes were produced at Sachsenhausen and were so good that they reflected great credit on all concerned.

At this point someone else came on the scene who knew a great deal more about life in Britain than their first adviser. He agreed that £5 notes were comparatively rare in Britain, but pointed out correctly that this made them quite unsuitable for general distribution. They aroused notice, he said. It was not too easy to get one changed except at a bank; even in a shop where one was known it was common to be asked to write one's name on the back before it would be accepted. If they suddenly appeared by scores in the hands of working-class people and country folk, a large rat would immediately be smelt and the only result would be that nobody in Britain would touch a "fiver" at any price, no, not from the hands of the Chief Cashier of the Bank of England in person. The German authorities sighed deeply and gave up the idea; why they never turned out ordinary one-pound and ten-shilling treasury notes instead, nobody knows.

The beautiful but useless notes more or less lay about at Sachsenhausen and a few people took them home as souvenirs or gave them to friends as curios. They got about Europe; men in the Occupation Forces in France and Italy found to their surprise that even in the middle of the war there were many people who put more faith in an English five-pound note than in German Occupation marks or even their own rocking currencies; this is, perhaps, the greatest compliment that Britain has ever been paid.

This curious fact came to the knowledge of Himmler and, through him, to the other leaders of the German Reich. Most of them were out for loot, headed by several lengths—or widths—by Goering and Ribbentrop. They wanted loot; if it was simply stolen there was trouble, besides which it was bad for discipline. Very well, let these things be bought with money which cost little to produce and the decencies of commerce would be approximately preserved. Magnificent.

Himmler set up groups of the Gestapo in each of the occupied countries to deal with this business. They bought valuables of all kinds; jewels, pictures, china, carvings, glass, furniture, carpets—anything beautiful and precious. If any seller was astute enough to notice something amiss with the notes and silly enough to say so, he was at once denounced as a Black Marketeer and removed to an elimination camp. The thing was simple.

The head of the Italian branch of this business was an enormous man named Van Hartmann, misshapen with fat and gross in mind and body. He said, when his happy days had passed and he stood before the Allied Intelligence Officers for interrogation, that he was a German descendant of a Dutch family. The point is not important, but neither is Van Hartmann; not now. In those days he was important. His headquarters were in the little town of Merano in the South Tyrol; since it was here that the Germans had established an assembly of military hospitals it was only sensible that Van Hartmann's office should masquerade as a branch of the International Red Cross. He was very well known, a fat kindly gentleman with a kindly comfortable wife; they really did visit hospitals and so did many of their staff, reading to the wounded, writing their letters for them and doing their shopping in the clean white town. But it was all a sham, Van Hartmann had no more connection with the International Red Cross in Geneva than the grand organ in St. Peter's in Rome has with a street barrel-organ complete with monkey. Van Hartmann's other hobby was antiques. Why not?

He was also well known in Milan, though here he had no connection with any Red Cross. Here he was just a buyer of antiques and his principal assistant was his wife, not the large comfortable lady of Merano but a slim young woman. Not so young, when looked at closely, as she appeared at first sight; she had smooth fair hair and hard blue eyes, and wore the badge of the Hitler Youth.

Van Hartmann's purchases went to Germany in special trucks with strong locks upon the doors. They were returned to him not quite empty, they usually contained cases of the good German delicatessen his soul loved, also champagne and a barrel or so of lager. There were heavy delays on the railways in those days due to the disgusting activities of the British and American bomber squadrons. Upon one such occasion the expected trucks were ten days late, Van Hartmann was eager for their arrival because he had a large consignment ready to go back. Also, he had run out of beer. At last the stationmaster at Milan rang up Van Hartmann's palatial flat and said that two trucks had arrived that afternoon.

"Two? Only two? There should be four."

"Tomorrow," said the stationmaster soothingly. "Doubtless tomorrow they will come."

"You have been saying that every day for the past week," snapped Van Hartmann, and replaced the receiver.

"Hilde!" he called. "Hilde, two trucks are at the station. Only two."

His Milan wife came into the room and said that two were better than nothing especially if they contained beer.

"I shall go down and see about it," said Van Hartmann.

"I will come with you," she said.

When they reached the goods yard the two trucks in question had been shunted alongside a rough concrete platform and the stationmaster and one of the goods porters were standing by looking at them.

"There are probably some cases inside for me," said Van Hartmann.

"There is something alive inside this one, with respect," said the stationmaster. "Listen!"

There were, indeed, scrambling noises inside and a voice engaged in some kind of monologue.

"Open the door!" said Van Hartmann, and it was done. The open doorway framed the figure of a dishevelled young man on hands and knees, his face was blackened with smoke and dust, his brown hair hung over his forehead in streaks and his eyes did not appear to focus. He blinked in the strong sunlight and shuffled back a little.

"Come out!" roared Van Hartmann. He spoke in Italian but the young man replied in French.

"Before I decide to come out," he said, slurring his words, "I sh'd liketer know—whereiam?"

"With respect," said the stationmaster, "the passenger appears to be inebriated," and Hilde laughed.

"Drag him out and put him under the tap," said Van Hartmann. Urged by the porter the passenger came out with a rush, when he was seen to be holding a bottle in his left hand. A tall bottle with the remains of gold foil round its neck, and it was empty. Van Hartmann snatched it from him.

"My champagne! This variegated animal has had the colossal impudence to dare to drink my champagne. You shall regret this, debased animal that you are——"

"Perhaps he had nothing else to drink," suggested Hilde.

"Then he could have died. What? A miserable Frenchman to steal my wine? He shall die now, anyway."

"I am not so sure," said Hilde coolly, and strolled along the little platform to the shed at the end. Here was a tap on the end of a short length of pipe against the shed wall; the stationmaster and the porter had got the passenger's head under it and were industriously rinsing it.

"I should think that would do," said Hilde. "Stand him up; I want to look at him."

They stood him up against the wall, she looked carefully at him and then nodded.

"That will do," she said, and returned to Van Hartmann. He was inside the van and swearing fluently because the cases had all been broken open and there was very little left.

"He has even tapped the beer," he wailed, "look, with a nail pushed through the bung. It will be a far-from-adequate punishment when he is shot as a saboteur tomorrow morning."

"He will not be shot," said Hilde distinctly.

The German put his head out of the doorway and said: "Not shot? Who says so when I order it?"

"I do."

"Oh? And why?"

"Because I want him."

"What for?"

"I think he will be useful," she said, turning to walk away. "So he will not be shot," she added over her shoulder. "He will be brought to the flat and I will see to him." She walked slowly along the platform and out of sight with Van Hartmann staring after her. His features were so blurred with fat that the expression on his face normally varied but little; this time an acute observer would have said that he was afraid.

When the passenger opened his eyes next morning he saw an attic bedroom with whitewashed walls and the minimum of furniture. There was, however, a bed and he was comfortably tucked up in it. Wherever he was, whatever this place was, it was certainly not a prison. He remembered nothing of his arrival at Milan station the previous evening, and he had not been able to see the name of any station on the journey. He remembered travelling in a truck for what seemed like months but was actually eight days, and now he was in a room, in bed. Well, it was an immense improvement on the truck. He yawned and went to sleep again.

He was awakened later by the sound of a key being turned in a lock. The door of his room opened and a woman walked in. She stood by his bed and looked down at him, he stared up at her and much of his natural impudence deserted him.

"So you are awake, at last."

"Yes, madame, thank you. Is it permitted to ask where I am?"

"You are in Milan. This is the flat of the Herr Van Hartmann. I am Frau Van Hartmann. Who are you?"

"I am Pierre Guyon, madame, greatly in your debt. I——"

"Papers?"

"In my coat pocket on that chair. Permit me——" But she had them out of the pocket before he could move and took them across to the window, for the light was failing a little.

"Pierre Guyon, of Paris, of French nationality. You say that?"

"But, naturally, madame. My papers——"

"But, naturally," she mimicked, "these papers are forgeries. For one thing, they say that you are a carpenter by trade. Now, I think you are an art dealer."

He retired under the bedclothes as far as possible, leaving only a pair of terrified brown eyes above the sheet. She nodded thoughtfully and went on talking.

"I think you were one of those dealers who made their living selling faked pictures. A picture is stolen from some gallery, is it not, and while it is still missing it is copied and sold several times over to different collectors in foreign countries. Then the original is returned to the gallery. That is one scheme, is it not? The buyers are in no position to complain since they had no business to buy it in the first place. Eh?"

He recovered a little courage. "If they do, madame, one tells them that they have the original and that it is a copy which has been returned to the gallery."

" They must be good copies."

"They are, madame. Only the real experts can tell, and even they are sometimes mistaken. Besides, a picture obtained in that manner is not shown to experts."

"But you are an expert yourself?"

"I am not in the first rank, madame," he said, with un-accustomed modesty, "but I have had experience."

"I believe you. You gained a little more experience of a different kind, did you not, when you sold three faked pictures to the agents of the Herr Reichsmarschall Goering. His experts were definitely in the first rank, I understand. What did you do then?"

He did not dare to lie to this terrifying woman who appeared to know as much about him as the Recording Angel. "I changed my name, burned all my papers, madame, obtained a new set—those you have there—and moved to another part of Paris."

"And so escaped arrest."

"Yes, madame."

"Continue."

"There was a round-up in my district for workers in German factories and I was caught. They sent us in a train to Germany via Brussels; just outside Brussels we were stopped for a long time, there was an air-raid and the track was damaged. The train doors were all supposed to be locked but I found one that was not. There was also a long train of goods waggons drawn up on the track next to our train. I took a water-bottle and two haversacks of rations—the corridor was full of luggage of all kinds—and stepped out of my train. I found the truck in which I travelled, the doors were not quite closed and I saw sacks and matting wrappers inside which would serve for a bed. I hid under them. Presently someone came along and locked the doors, soon after that the train started. I knew that truck was going to Italy by the labels on the cases, I thought I would wait till it was well down in the South of France and then slip away. It was then, madame, that I

discovered the impossibility of opening the door——"
His voice died away artistically and he closed his eyes as
though the memory of that moment were more than he
could bear.

"So you drowned your anxieties in the Herr Van Hartmann's champagne," said Hilde briskly.

"Yes," he said frankly. There was no sense in attempt-
ing denial.

"For which he proposes to have you shot."

"Madame!"

"Well? What else would you expect?"

"I expect nothing, madame. I may perhaps be permitted
to found a small hope upon madame's evident goodness
of heart." She did not look as though she had as much
goodness of heart as the average tigress but he had been
brought to her house, washed, undressed and put to bed
like a Christian. Why do that if he were only to be shot?

"I might have a use for you if you really know as much
about pictures as you suggest. The Herr Van Hartmann
and I are ourselves interested in the purchase of antiques——" She paused and he realized that she meant
"for the Germans." He nodded and she went on: "I
could do with a man who would advise me honestly and
faithfully about pictures. I think you are intelligent
enough to see that it will pay you to be both honest and
faithful. Otherwise, of course, the Herr Reichsmarschall
might learn to whom he owes his spurious Monets. Eh?"

"Madame, I will serve you as a devout Catholic serves
his——"

"I will see that you do, thank you. I will take these
papers of yours, you will remember that it is an additional
offence for you to have had them. I will give you Ger-

man papers and yet another name. You will start work tomorrow."

He began to thank her but she walked out of the room as though he had not spoken and locked the door behind her. He sat up in bed as though he were stifling for air.

"I would do this," he murmured. "Escape from one lot of these culture racketeers and arrive in the arms of another lot. Of course, my description has been sent round to every office—how thoroughly German to be so thorough—and she recognized me. Well, I'm not dead yet."

He served the Van Hartmann concern faithfully and well until the time came when the Allies advanced through Italy, the German resistance was hammered down and at last they surrendered. When it was finally obvious that all was lost there was a sort of company meeting to wind up the Van Hartmann concern.

"It is quite useless," said Van Hartmann, "for me to attempt escape. For one thing, I am too well known, for another——" he glanced down at his increasing corpulence—"I have not the figure for it."

"No," said Hilde clearly. "That, my dear, is obvious. But I see no reason why I should stay to hold your hand in captivity. I shall——"

"They wouldn't let you, anyway," he said with something like a chuckle. "Very moral people, our enemies. Women are kept in jails separate from all men. Even their husbands, my love."

The young man who had once called himself Pierre Guyon was in the room, standing respectfully near the door. He noticed with interest that the fat man was not, at least at that moment, so depressed at his impending ruin as one would expect. He was nearly cheerful; there was a strongly compensating circumstance somewhere and the young man wondered what it was. The facade of affectionate unity between the Van Hartmanns had cracked once or twice in his presence, there had been disagreements and arguments in which Hilde had always won and the fat man climbed down. Why?

"There is that house I bought in Belgium," said Hilde. "I have a good background there. I shall apply to be sent back home, they are returning all expatriated workers. I will take Pierre with me, it will add colour to my story. Another victim of German aggression, you know."

"Pierre?"

She indicated the young man by the door. "Pierre Guyon. He called himself that when he came, if you remember. It is a good thing I kept his papers, they will be useful now. Can I have that picture?"

She pointed at a small Matisse hanging on the wall above Van Hartmann's desk, he turned and looked up at it.

"Certainly, my dear, take it. Anything else?"

"No, it would not be safe, but I can hide this. I always liked it."

She went out of the room with the picture in her hands and Van Hartmann watched her out of sight.

"At least," he said in a half-whisper, "at least it will not matter now that I have a Jewish grandfather."

He slumped down in his chair with eyes half closed, looking at nothing; the young man waited a moment and then tiptoed quietly out of the room.

II

THE MAN WHO WAS AFRAID

HAMBLEDON came out of the doorway of the Hotel Albert Premier at the corner of the Place Rogier in Brussels; behind him the hotel porter carried two suitcases and suggested calling a station porter. He received no reply and repeated the remark.

"What?" said Hambledon. "No, I don't think so, thanks."

"And m'sieu's luggage?"

"I'll carry it."

"On so hot an evening, m'sieu'?"

Hambledon hesitated.

"Put my bags inside again for the moment, please. I'll call back for them."

The porter nodded and took the suitcases inside the hotel; Hambledon lit a cigarette and strolled irresolutely away. There was a line of cars parked with their bonnets towards the pavement, he passed between two of them and hesitated again. But no man crosses the Rue de Brabant irresolutely and lives, three cars shot past his nose at forty miles an hour and Hambledon woke up. He waited for a gap in the traffic and ran for the open space in the middle of the square. There was a cafe diagonally opposite, he would have a cup of coffee there and make up his mind one way or the other. There were plenty of trains to Antwerp.

The cafe was half empty at that hour of the evening, Hambledon sat at a table just inside the open windows. The waiter brought the coffee in the usual tin percolator with a glass mug underneath, Hambledon sat waiting while the brown liquid dripped through. He had been in Brussels for a fortnight trying to uncover some trace of the organization which was flooding Western Europe with forged notes; there was known to be a distributing centre somewhere in Belgium and it was believed to be in Brussels. The Belgian police in all its branches had been most helpful; other sources of information had been filtered as thoroughly as the coffee; Hambledon himself had done all that a lifetime of guile and resource could suggest, but not a spark glimmered in the darkness to show that they were anywhere near the right track. Hambledon sighed, removed the percolator from the top of the mug and set it down in its inverted lid upon one of the cardboard mats which Continental cafes provide in such plenty. As a rule they advertise the local beer on one side, the under side is blank and visitors with the party spirit sign their names on the blank side and post them to envious friends at home. The mats in the Taverne Gruber advertised Cristal Alken; Hambledon glanced at them without interest and went on thinking.

Wherever there is paper currency there will be forged notes, but usually only upon a small scale. Two or three men of great skill and patience will produce the paper, engrave the plates and print the notes; a dozen more will distribute them; only enough are made to keep these few in comfort and provide for their old age. One does not wish to draw attention to oneself by attaining the dimensions of a National Mint. But that was exactly what was happening at the moment, currency notes were being turned out somewhere in quantities so inordinate as to have become a menace to the financial stability of the countries attacked. French francs, American dollar bills, Dutch guilders, Belgian francs, English Treasury and Bank notes, all of excellent quality, were drifting along in quantities which were causing the gravest anxiety to the various national Exchequers. "Damn it," said Hambledon, "they must have a factory as big as Ford's." He stirred up the sugar in his coffee and sipped it. The French made a good haul in Marseilles a few months ago but of course they only got a few of the distributors. The notes were not being printed in France.

Hambledon shifted in his chair and glanced at his watch. That Antwerp train had gone but it didn't matter, there would be another in half an hour's time. He would give up Brussels and try Antwerp; it was, after all, a seaport town, and for that reason perhaps more probable. It would not matter if he arrived late, his room was booked.

He threw his depressing meditations from him and looked with interest at the scene before him. While he had been sitting there the twilight had deepened and all over Brussels the lights were on; Brussels, now more the *Ville Lumière* than Paris. Neon lights all round the Place Rogier in all colours, red and blue and green; against the sky the huge revolving searchlight on the roof of the Bon Marche is visible fifty miles away when you come by air from Paris. The pavements were filling with people strolling along in the warm evening, girls in light summer frocks and men with their coats open, usually hatless.

The Taverne Gruber was beginning to fill up and there rose that babble of mixed tongues which Hambledon loved. The French of Paris and the French of Belgium which sounds quite different, three men near by arguing hotly in Italian, two girls at the next table talking Flemish, a clear English voice above the others: "My dear, the Customs man will simply hurl me into jail!" The waiters wriggled between the tables with trays or rushed to the bar with shouted orders. *"Trois filtres! Deux Exports!"* The place grew even warmer and smelt of coffee, wine and perfumes; a happy scene, thought Hambledon, and relaxed comfortably.

A young man came into the cafe and made straight for a vacant table, usually the last to be occupied as it was awkwardly placed, Hambledon noticed him because unlike the others he was not happy; he was worried and anxious. He was a thin young man shabbily dressed, not well shaven, with deep lines from his nose to the corners of his mouth, and his eyes too near together. Not an attractive person. He signalled the waiter and gave an order; while he was waiting he looked quickly and furtively about him, sitting low in his chair in order not to be conspicuous. It dawned upon Hambledon that the man was not merely anxious, he was afraid.

The waiter came back with a glass of beer and set it down on the cardboard mat in front of the young man. He sipped his beer; apparently noticing the mat for the first time he pushed it round with his finger to read the advertisement on the face. He then glanced round to see if anyone was watching him, turned the mat over and looked at the back. There was something written on it, Hambledon was sure of it. There was no mistaking the little frown of concentration. The man dropped the mat on the table again, keeping his fingers carelessly upon it, a moment later he slipped it into his pocket.

Hambledon was interested. Of course, people did scribble on these cards, usually mathematical problems dealing with currency. If Belgian francs are 176 to the English pound, how much is a glass of port? But no one pockets such scribbled figures as these; this was something more. However, the young man sat still and drank his beer; Hambledon turned his attention to the scene outside.

Three of the tall buildings round the Place Rogier—one of them was his own hotel, the Albert Premier—had flood-lights on their roofs trained down upon the square and the place was as light as day even without the other illuminations. A man came hurrying across the square, dodging between the strolling people. He was in too much of a hurry to be careful, as he trotted across the road to the cafe a motor bus missed him by inches. The driver applied a well-chosen epithet but the man never turned his head; he slid, panting, between the tables outside the Gruber and came to a dead stop with his eyes upon the young man who had just pocketed the cardboard mat.

"Well, well," said Hambledon to himself, and ordered another coffee.

The man outside the door shrugged his shoulders, assumed an expression of resignation and prepared to wait. He was a middle-aged man but light and active in his movements, with a sallow lined face. He strolled restlessly about, a few paces either way. At the corner of the Place Rogier and the Avenue des Boulevards there stood a cigarette-seller with a tray hung from his shoulders;

there was always one there in the evenings after the shops closed. He just stood there, jostled by the passers-by, uttering at regular intervals a hoarse cry of "*Cigarettes! Chocolats!*" Hambledon bought cigarettes from him one night and was surprised to find that they were the normal price and not at Black Market rates.

The man who was waiting outside walked along to the cigarette-seller and bought a packet. He lit one and began to walk steadily up and down outside, looking in every time he passed. Evidently it was that particular table he wanted since there were others still vacant; equally plainly he was not interested in the younger man since he could have walked straight in and spoken to him. Was it too much, Hambledon asked himself, to assume that what the man outside wanted was the mat which the man inside had got? Hambledon suggested to himself that it was not, and settled down to wait for what came next. The inscription on the card, whatever it might be, was almost certainly not simple arithmetic.

At last the young man at the table finished his beer and signalled to the waiter; the older man outside left off patrolling to watch and Hambledon drank the last drops of his coffee. Would the man inside order another drink or merely pay the waiter? He paid, got up from his seat and walked out. The man outside entered as promptly, he actually passed the first man in the doorway without showing the faintest interest in him. The waiter was still by the table when the newcomer reached it, he ordered something and sat down. As soon as the waiter's back was turned the man turned over the cardboard mat in front of him and looked closely at the back. He threw it down and examined the other two mats, for on this table

26

there were only three where there had been four. He drummed with his fingers for a moment, made up his mind and walked quickly out. His whole act had taken so short a time that the first man was still in sight, walking slowly across the Place Rogier towards the entrance of the Rue de Brabant. The second man rushed after him and then slowed down in order not to overtake him.

Inside the cafe Hambledon stood up, signalled to the waiter, left a twenty-franc note for him, and walked out after the two men.

Outside the cafe, at the corner of the square, the man who had been selling cigarettes called in a low clear voice to a man who was standing by. "Emile!" he said, "you can have your tray back now." He slipped the strap over his head as he spoke, handed the tray to Emile and followed on behind the unsuspecting Hambledon.

A short distance up the Rue de Brabant a beautiful new concrete railway bridge crosses the road. It is to carry the railway line between the Nord and Midi stations, a line which is still under construction, and even the bridge was not quite finished when Hambledon was there. They had not put in the shops, small lock-up shops each enclosed within a semi-circular vault under the bridge and part of its construction. At this date the future shops were a row of caverns, most of them blocked up but one or two at the further end still open; dark, gritty, and smelling of damp concrete.

There were but few people about when the young man with the cardboard mat in his pocket reached the bridge and began to walk through it. The second man, who had hung back while they were in the brightly-lighted street, quickened his step and began to overhaul him. Hambledon, thirty yards behind, followed suit. He could see the two men quite well until a couple of cars came roaring down under the bridge and their headlights blinded him for a moment. When his sight cleared again the men were not to be seen anywhere in the considerable length ahead. There was only one place where they could be; Hambledon broke into a run.

When he came to the first arch which was not blocked up he stopped and looked in; the place was full of shadows but not quite dark and in the far corner he made out what looked like a bundle of sacks with someone bending over it. Hambledon uttered an exclamation at which the stooping man straightened up and immediately rushed out past him and away along the street till his running footsteps died in the distance. Tommy Hambledon made no attempt to stop him but switched on a small electric torch he carried and went forward to investigate the bundle of sacks. As he expected, it was the young man from the Cafe Gruber and he had been shot through the head.

Tommy looked round, remembering a metallic clatter when the murderer ran away. There was a small automatic lying on the ground and Hambledon pocketed it. He was unarmed and if the evening kept on as it had started a gun might be useful.

"I'd better leave," he thought, "if anyone comes along now I'll be in rather a spot. I wonder if he found that card, he hadn't much time——"

Hambledon remembered which pocket the card had been put into, he rolled the victim over. It was still there; Tommy dropped it into his own pocket and walked rapidly away. Not in the same direction as the running man whom he never wished to see again, but back towards the Place Rogier and his own hotel. Before he had quite cleared the bridge he met a man who, he thought, glanced at him sharply, but perhaps it was just his natural caution suggesting unpleasantnesses. This was a short fat man with a florid complexion and a small spiky moustache. He did not pause or speak and Hambledon went on his way.

The reception clerk at the Albert Premier hurried to bring Hambledon's suitcase from the luggage room, but Tommy said: "I've changed my mind about leaving to-night. Is there a room I can have? My own room again? Oh, splendid, that will feel just like home. I suppose I must fill up all those forms again—not even that? Better and better. No, I don't know how long I shall be staying, I will try to be a little more definite tomorrow."

The lift-man took Hambledon up to his room on the 3rd floor and carried his bags for him, remarking that it was indeed a pleasure that m'sieu' was not leaving them after all. Tommy, with his mind on the cardboard mat he had not yet had time to examine, uttered a couple of amiable grunts, rewarded the man and locked the door after him.

On the back of the card was written in French: "Parcel at 208 Rue Olive. Ask for Raoul."

"Yes," said Hambledon, tapping the card thoughtfully against his nose, "that's all very well, but does Raoul know whom to expect? I daresay I could talk my way out of it again, but it would perhaps be as well if somebody knew where I was going." He put the card down, rang through the house telephone to ask for coffee to be sent up to his room, and unlocked the door to admit the waiter when he came. In the meantime Hambledon amused himself by unpacking his things and putting them tidily back into the drawers. "It is, naturally, just a question of what is in the parcel. There is no sort of certainty that this business has any connection with those forged notes, but a parcel a man will commit murder to get should be an interesting parcel. Russian Crown jewels went out of circulation years ago. Of course it might contain the mummified head of Martin Bormann." He picked up the card again and looked at it. "One could at least walk past the house——"

There came a knock at the door. Hambledon, assuming it to be the waiter with his coffee, shouted: "Come in!" and turned to find himself looking down the barrel of an unpleasantly large revolver. The man who was holding it was the fat little man with a spiky moustache who had passed him under the railway bridge in the Rue de Brabant twenty minutes earlier. He sidled into the room, if such a rotund form could be said to sidle, and pushed the door shut behind him with his shoulder.

"Your pardon, m'sieu'," he said politely. "The hands up, if it will not inconvenience you."

"Who the hell are you?" asked Tommy indignantly, raising his hands as requested. He tried to slip the card up his sleeve but it was just too wide.

"It is a matter of no importance, my name. You have, I think, a cardboard mat from the Taverne Gruber in your possession. It is, if I mistake not, in your right hand at the moment. If you would have the goodness to toss it to me lightly I should be infinitely obliged."

Hambledon did not include the card among the things for which it is obligatory to risk one's life and anyway he had memorized the address. He threw it across and his visitor caught it, glanced at the message and dropped the card in his pocket. He then leaned back against the door and addressed Hambledon in a conversational tone.

"It would be of the greatest interest to me to know your name but I am not of a credulity so innocent as to think that it would assist me to ask you. Yet," he added thoughtfully, "it is necessary to be just. You do not look like one of the crooks from the Marine Cat——"

"The what?"

"The Marine Cat. I see you are not; that look of surprise, it is genuine or I will go back to school. None the less, I have seen your face before, I cannot place it, it is exasperating, that. No matter, it will come. So that is the place for tonight."

"What is, my face?"

"No, no. Not at all. 208 Rue Olive, as written on that card."

"Presumably," said Hambledon drily. "I am sure you need no instruction from me."

"I fear I shall not obtain it. I have, in my time, made mistakes, m'sieu'—not many, but some—but the rosy optimism, she is not among them. Who is Yanni's aunt?"

"How you do leap about," complained Hambledon. "Who, to begin at the beginning, is Yanni?"

"It is true that I heard him called that but it may not be his name. He who lies dead under the arch of that bridge."

"Oh, him," began Hambledon, and at that moment there came a knock at the door. "My coffee at last."

The visitor sprang away from the door to stand beside Hambledon, in the same instant the gun disappeared from sight and Tommy dropped his arms. "You will give me that revolver," he added.

The revolver changed hands and Hambledon called to the waiter to come in. "Bring another cup," he added, "for my friend here. He needs it."

"At once, m'sieu'," said the waiter alertly, and left the room.

"Now that matters have been more suitably arranged," said Hambledon, showing the large revolver, "I want to see your papers. If not genuine they will at least throw some light upon what you are pretending to be."

"I am not pretending at all, I am Antoine Letord of the Sûreté and this is my card."

"I am not altogether surprised," said Hambledon. "There was something in your manner which struck a familiar note. I am Hambledon of British Intelligence."

"Ah," said Letord, "I remember now. You were a guest at the Sûreté whom everyone delighted to honour. Accept my apologies which are, indeed, from the heart. I knew I had seen your distinguished features before but I was mentally turning over the pages of the rogues' gallery I carry here——" he tapped his head—"it is no wonder I could not find you."

"Tell me," said Hambledon, "how you knew I was here? I think you did not follow me from the railway bridge."

"I have been in Brussels some time," said Letord. "Then you come and begin to frequent the Taverne Gruber. Those others also do that and I wondered. I noticed that you lived here, at the Albert, I found that interesting. I say to myself that we do not find the *sous-officiers* of crime staying in an *hotel du premier ordre*, is it

32

possible that at last I encounter someone of importance? So I acquire information and the name I saw was not Hambledon——"

"I thought perhaps better not——"

"Precisely. M'sieu' is, as always, justified. That is all, except that when Yanni went out with Burenne after him and you upon the heels of Burenne I say to myself: 'Antoine! Forward.' I accordingly returned the tray of cigarettes to the man from whom I borrowed it—it cost me a hundred francs and I can but hope the Department will pay—and followed after. You know what I saw, though I was not sure who—forgive me—had shot Yanni."

"Don't apologize," said Hambledon. "Yanni looked the sort who does tend to get shot sooner or later. Burenne? He was a good deal older than Yanni, wasn't he?"

"Burenne comes from Paris and that is partly why I am here. We thought he might help us over a certain matter but he did not desire to co-operate. No. He came to Brussels so I came too." Letord looked at Hambledon. "I have no wish to intrude upon m'sieu's reasons for being here, but——"

"Forged currency. And you?"

"The same, yes. Burenne had a knife in that pâté we think."

"And, while we are clearing up, the Marine Cat?"

"Just a cafe where crooks go. I was there today. Also Yanni, also a drunk man who talked. He told Yanni a muddled story about a mat at the Gruber, it would seem the poor Yanni knew enough to make sense of it. I also, that is why I was selling cigarettes. In effect, I wished very much to see who wrote the message but there I failed, had you any better fortune, m'sieu'?"

Hambledon shook his head. "I knew nothing of any message till I saw Yanni pocket it. No one sat at that table before him while I was there. The message was meant for Burenne, of course. Just one thing more—who is Yanni's aunt?"

"I do not know. He is called Yanni the Nephew, that is all. 'Here comes the Nephew,' when he approaches, and 'Hola, Yanni, how's your aunt?' He smiles and makes no reply."

"Just a joke, perhaps," said Hambledon. "Possibly rude."

III

PAPA

"BY the way," said Hambledon, "I have one thing here to show you. Burenne's automatic, he dropped it when he ran away and I picked it up. Taking one thing with another I thought it would be better in my pocket than in his. Here it is."

The French detective waved it away. "I think it will still be better in your pocket, m'sieu', for the present. It is true it could be evidence that that is the gun which fired the shot into Yanni, but that is for the Belgian police, not us. I have already enough on my plate without agitating myself about the murder of Yanni." He swept Yanni away with a gesture. "One thing I have, his fingerprints. I paused for that only before following m'sieu'. I have here a small apparatus of my own invention." He produced from his pocket a flat metal case. "A photographic dark slide, as you see, with a plate in it, but not for photography. No. The emulsion side I keep damp; when I wish for the prints of someone unconscious or dead I pull the slide out, press the fingers on the emulsion, and I have it. Besides, it does not mark the fingers so no one knows it has been done. My idea, m'sieu'."

"How often," said Hambledon, "have I been told not to touch the emulsion or I shall fingermark it, and I never thought of that. It is genius, that. You thought Yanni's might be useful?"

Letord shrugged his shoulders. "It is only if he is in the Records; now we know he is dead, that is all."

There came a knock at the door; the waiter with Letord's coffee, and Hambledon laughed.

"Are you sure you really wish for that? I seem to remember that I did not consult you. A glass of wine, perhaps——"

But Letord preferred coffee and the waiter went away.

"And now," said Hambledon, "what is, in your opinion, our next move?"

"This parcel," said Letord. He sat down on one of Hambledon's chairs and arranged his feet upon another. "If m'sieu' will excuse. The feet, they are hard-working servants. They deserve consideration. This parcel at the house in the Rue Olive."

"Yes," said Hambledon. "I had myself arrived at precisely that point when you—when you presented me with the honour of your acquaintance. Correct me now if I am wrong. Burenne does not know the address since he had no opportunity to read the card. Yes. Next, this house in the Rue Olive; it's an accommodation address, isn't it? The people who live there, they are merely carriers, go-betweens, aren't they? Is that your opinion also?"

"I know nothing of the house and still less of those who live there. I should, however, be agreeably surprised to find them innocent, and in my trade, m'sieu', the surprises are seldom agreeable. They know what they are doing, that company. As to what you say of their unimportance, I have no means of knowing."

"The point I was trying to make," said Hambledon, "is

this. Is it likely that they are expecting Burenne or would know him if they saw him?"

"They will probably be expecting somebody tonight. As to whether they know whom to expect——"

"We know these organizations, you and I. The head of it is one man, or two or three who more or less trust each other——"

"Usually because any one of them is in the happy position of being able to put the others in jail," said Letord with his quick grin.

"Precisely. But the rank and file they do not trust at all, and rightly. Liars, rogues and double-crossers every one. From this there arise these elaborate arrangements, of which this beer-card business is typical, for passing messages without any personal contact between one man and another. I suggest to you again, my dear m'sieu' Letord, that Burenne was going as a stranger to the house of strangers——"

Letord burst out laughing. "I see one thing very plainly, m'sieu' Hambledon, it is that you have determined already to go to this house yourself and nobody shall stop you."

"It is true that I had already told myself that it would be a good idea to go there provided somebody knew where I had gone, and here are you like an answer to prayer. But it may be that you have some better reason for going there yourself?"

"I have a very good reason for staying away," said Letord frankly. "It is that it has for many years been my business to pursue criminals, and it may be that the man who shall open the door of that house is one with whom I have had my affairs before. Then the little mice will all run away down their holes and the poor cat can just fold up his tail and go home."

Hambledon nodded. "It is settled, then. I will go to the house in the Rue Olive. If I don't return within a reasonable time, you will——"

"I am coming with you, but not inside. It may be that some immediate action may be necessary and I, Antoine Letord, will provide it."

Twenty minutes later Hambledon arrived at the house in question. It was, he was pleased to notice, one of a row of similar small houses joined together; they did not look as though the intervening walls would be particularly thick, it would not be possible to start any very noisy sort of trouble—firing revolvers, for example—without the neighbours being aware of it. Nor did these seem the sort of houses where the neighbours do not mind guns being fired or people being thrown from windows. They were not rich, these tenants, but they had their self-respect. Curtains were clean and doorsteps whitened. He knocked at the door and saw, as he stepped back, the stout form of Letord drifting aimlessly into a cafe on the other side of the road.

The door opened suddenly and a man looked out, an elderly man with his shirtsleeves rolled up and his braces dangling. Hambledon had interrupted his toilet, evidently, for the man's face was partly lathered and he held a shaving-brush in his right hand. He looked at Hambledon but did not speak.

"I have called to fetch a parcel," said Tommy, "if it is not inconveniencing you. I was told to say that Raoul would know all about it."

The man continued to look at Hambledon and gave

himself two or three absent-minded pokes with the shaving-brush. He then opened the door wider and said: "Come in." He led the way along the passage, passing the foot of the stairs, and into a room at the back of the house. He indicated a chair against the wall and told Hambledon to sit down, "it is necessary to wait a little."

The room was plainly a kitchen; there was a sink at the further end, a large tiled stove, a dresser with miscellaneous crockery, and a table in the middle of the room at which a short solid girl was standing, ironing blouses. The elderly man walked across to the sink and went on lathering his face, the girl glanced at Hambledon and did not speak. The only sounds in the room were the small splashing noises from the sink, the bump-bump of the girl's iron, and a faint simmering noise from a pot on the top of the stove. A long minute passed and the silence became embarrassing, Hambledon cleared his throat and shifted his feet; the man looked over his shoulder towards him.

"What a nice stove," said Tommy, and it was quite true.

The man turned from the sink and came towards him. "It is a nice stove," he agreed. "Of good quality."

"New, too," said Hambledon, "surely."

"No, no. That stove is not new. It must be—what—twelve years old. Yes, quite twelve years old."

"One would scarcely credit it," said Tommy. "The tiles, every one complete, not even a cracked one."

"It has had great care taken of it," said the man, and looked reproachfully at his shaving-brush. "The lather, it dries, you understand," he said, and returned to the sink. The girl folded up one blouse and started on another, Hambledon sat still and thought this was one of the oddest houses he was ever in. The silence settled down again only to be broken a few minutes later by a most peculiar noise. It came from somewhere outside the house, a rhythmical chanting which ran up and down the scale, and Tommy sat up.

"That noise," he said, "what is it?"

The girl looked up from her ironing. "It is the Jews, m'sieu'."

"Oh, is it? A near-by synagogue, I suppose," and she nodded.

A moment later the door opened and a second girl came in, a tall young woman with a thin haggard face. The man at the sink turned round.

"You two girls," he said, with some reaching after joviality, "can put on your hats and coats and go out."

"What, now?" asked the tall one. "It's early yet."

"Better go now," said the man. "Run along when I tell you."

Both girls glanced at Hambledon and it was plain that they assumed a connection between his presence and their absence. They did not argue; the one who had been ironing set up her iron on its heel on the tin lid she was using for a stand, picked up the finished blouse and walked out of the room. The tall one turned in the doorway to ask what about locking the front door, and the man said that when they were ready he would come and let them out. "Be quick," he added, picked up his razor and began, very slowly, to shave. Hambledon was quite relieved at this; the solemn persistent lathering had gone on so long that it had almost ceased to be a preliminary to further action and become a rite in itself. A sort of spell for the revival of youth might well start with a ritual removal of beard and whiskers, but youth festivals belong to Spring and this was October. Or perhaps the lather might have been put on to serve as a mask. Or persisted with as a signal to someone outside the further window: "Come in when I pick up my razor," and then what? But apparently the poor man was just plain slow.

He had got the hair off one side of his face when the tapping of high-heeled shoes on the stairs outside suggested that the girls were ready to go out. The man laid down his razor, muttered something about a key, and went out of the room, shutting the door behind him. There was a murmur of voices in the passage but no distinguishable words and presently the front door shut audibly. Immediately thereafter Hambledon heard the single stroke of a bell as when a telephone receiver is lifted, but still no audible speech.

Presently the door of the room opened again and the man came back, but not alone. Another man followed him, a swarthy young man in the rough clothes of a market porter, but instead of a basket of vegetables he carried a revolver which he levelled at Hambledon's head.

"Oh, really," said Hambledon, with pardonable irritation, "not another one?" He spoke in French and the young man understood him.

"What other one? Who are you? Hands up!"

Hambledon obeyed, summoning his very considerable dignity. "I am he who has been instructed to call here for a parcel, mentioning the name Raoul. Will you be so good as to stop flourishing that ridiculous cannon and give me the parcel? I have other business on hand tonight."

The young man laughed unpleasantly while the incredible old man actually wandered back to the sink and went on shaving.

"You are not he who was to come," said the man with the gun.

"I am not he who was originally to have come," explained Hambledon in a tone of strained patience, "but he was prevented from coming and therefore I am here instead."

"So we have been told already. We were expecting somebody like you. We deal with people like you. Papa!"

The man at the sink grunted.

"To the warehouse," added the young man. "You can finish shaving later. Get your coat on, quick."

Papa wiped most of the remaining soap off his face, leaving a sort of hangman's frill round the circumference, wriggled into his braces and put on his coat. He did not look at Hambledon nor appear particularly interested in the proceedings, which made it all the more shocking when he pulled a small pistol out of his pocket and advanced upon Hambledon.

"Look here, Papa," said Tommy in a scandalized tone, "you're too old for this sort of thing, you are really. Consider your grey hairs."

The young man told Hambledon in a rude phrase to shut his trap and added an epithet which was even ruder. "See if he's got a gun," he added. "The arms straight up, you!"

The older man found Burenne's automatic at once and looked at it dubiously.

"I do not understand these things, me," he complained.

"I do. Give it to me—put it in my pocket, so. Now then, march!"

They pushed Hambledon out of the room and down the passage into the street.

"I lock the door," said the householder, and turned to do so while Hambledon looked anxiously for Letord who was nowhere to be seen. There was, in fact, no one to be seen, the street was ominously empty.

"The neighbours, it appears," said Tommy conversationally, "are minding their own business."

"The neighbours have sense in their heads," said the young man, "unlike some people one meets. Put your hands down!" he added, for Hambledon was holding them above his head in the hope that some law-abiding person might see him and do something helpful. The old man turned away from the door, pushing a large key into his pocket. He resumed control of the pistol which he had tucked under his left arm like a newspaper and presented it at Hambledon's ribs. Close together, like friends, the three men strolled slowly along the pavement with Tommy in the middle retarding the pace as much as he dared. Letord had spoken of providing immediate action and now seemed the moment for it.

There came from behind them a padding sound as of people running in soft-soled shoes, it came nearer and the three men looked over their shoulders as a small crowd of men rounded the corner from the synagogue and spread into the road, running silently except for a hoarse grunt from the leaders and a gesture towards Hambledon and his escort. They were all men, younger ones in front and older men behind; among them Tommy recognized the stout figure of Letord pattering along with quick short steps and holding his hat on with one hand.

"The Jews!" said the old man, and backed against the house front, but the next moment the crowd was upon them and they all went down together. For Hambledon the moment was one of extreme confusion; not sure whether he was being murdered or rescued he went down under a heap of struggling bodies and expected a knife in him at any moment. He felt himself being dragged out by the feet and sat up, gasping. There was a loud bang close to his ear as the young man fired off his big revolver, the crack was followed by howls and yells of anger and, from a little further off, the blowing of police whistles. Letord let go of Tommy's ankles, seized him by the arm and lifted him to his feet. "Run," said the detective, and pulled him away. "Are you hurt? No, then run! Run!"

They turned the first corner they came to, ran down that street, round another corner, and another. Hambledon noticed with surprise that Letord could run much faster than one would expect, to look at him.

"Can't we walk now?" said Tommy, when the sounds of conflict had died away in the distance, but Letord stopped abruptly, clapped his hand to his forehead and called himself several species of imbecile. He turned on his heel and started back the way they had come. "Run! Run! There may yet be time!"

"Back again?" said Hambledon, cantering along behind him. "Whatever for?"

"The parcel," panted Letord. "The house is empty and the parcel is in the house." He put on a spurt and Hambledon drew level with him.

"But the street is full of people," he began.

44

"Back way," gasped Letord. "Through here."

He led the way to the synagogue, down a passage at the side and into a small yard. "That's the house," he said, "you were in that room. The blind was torn, I could see in. Now we open this window."

The window was not latched; as they climbed over the sill Hambledon said what a pleasure it was to work with the liberal-minded Continental police. "At home, if I broke into a house after this fashion I should almost certainly be arrested. That is, if I acted without the most careful precautions."

"But, regrettable," said Letord. "Deplorable, to be so hampered. At the same time I will point out to m'sieu' that we are not at the moment in France. We will not, I think, switch on the lights; the neighbours, you know. You have your torch, yes. You take that side of the room, I take this. The parcel, it will not be so small, and the greatest speed is desirable."

The house had only six rooms and was not overfull of furniture; in a quarter of an hour they had gone through it in sufficient detail to be fairly certain that no sizeable parcel was concealed in it. Hambledon gathered that the parcel would be about two feet long and a foot thick; "they are not notes of large denominations, you understand," said Letord, "such as would awaken suspicion when offered. Fifty or hundred-franc notes only, so there will be very many of them. Yes. They are not hidden in the coffee-pot, these samples."

Hambledon was peeping carefully from behind the curtains of a first-floor window. "The gendarmes are coming," he said. "We leave, don't we?"

They left very hurriedly by the same window which had

given them access, crossed the yard and trotted along the passage by the synagogue. "Now," said Letord, "run!"

"Oh dear no," said Hambledon, "not again. Walk, just walk. Or somebody will say 'why are these men running? Have they, then, painful consciences?' Then somebody will enquire into our consciences and that I cannot have. Besides, the weather is hot and I have run enough for one night."

Letord grinned and dropped into a walk. They put a couple of hundred yards between them and the synagogue and came to a cafe, not perhaps of the first class but brightly lit and cheerful.

"Beer," said Hambledon, pausing in his stride.

"*Vermouth cassis*," said Letord. They wheeled, shoulder to shoulder, and sat down at a small table on the pavement. The beer came, also the *vermouth cassis*, which is a drink composed of a dash of vermouth, an inch of blackcurrant syrup and a lot of sodawater, and contentment supervened.

"Tell me," said Tommy, "how did you manage to arrive so opportunely with your—your cohorts?"

"I went round the corner into the street behind," said Letord. "I thought there might be an alley at the back of that house, I found the path past the synagogue. There was a sort of service going on inside and several young Jews were standing about outside. They took no notice of me. I found that yard and peered in at the window. All went well, it seemed, the old one shaved himself and you waited. Presently the old one went out and came back with a man with a gun. I say to myself: 'Antoine, the moment for action is here. Act, then.' I run back down the passage and tell the Jews there is one of The Chosen Race

46

about to be assassinated. I cry: 'To the rescue! Remember the eleventh of August!' They call out their fellows and there is the rescue. That's all."

"I am more obliged to you than I can ever tell you," said Hambledon sincerely. "If it hadn't been for you—tell me, this eleventh of August business, what was it?"

"I haven't the least idea," said Letord. "But nor had they, so it didn't matter. What is this crowd, now?"

It was a loose crowd of people spreading across the street and milling round a small group in the middle. They came nearer; the group in the middle consisted of four gendarmes with two prisoners a good deal the worse for wear. The old man from the Rue Olive, still half-shaven, was limping and had a handkerchief tied round his head; the younger man who had menaced Hambledon with the big revolver had one arm in a sling and was holding his jaw with the other hand, there was blood running from a cut on his head. The crowd was mainly composed of Jews; remarks in various languages, including Yiddish, were being passed and they were not blessings.

Hambledon and Letord withdrew behind a potted palm and watched the procession pass. Two or three men detached themselves from the parade and dropped into the cafe for a drink, Hambledon accosted one of them.

"What is all this? What have those men done?"

"Arrested for shooting up some Jews, they've wounded several of them. Can't have that sort of thing in Brussels."

"I have seen those two prisoners before," said Letord in a slow clear voice. "Earlier this evening. They were with a third man where the new railway bridge crosses the Rue de Brabant. They hustled him into one of the open arches and there were noises. . . . Only those two men came out again."

"What? You saw that? In the Rue de Brabant?" The man gulped down his beer and stood up. "The police must be told of this. Come on, Piet."

He and his friend ran down the street after the procession and Hambledon looked at Letord.

"When they search him they'll find the gun that killed Yanni," he said. "And the police will require our evidence."

"Precisely," said Letord, and rose to his feet. "I think we walk again a little, do we not?"

"Walk?" said Hambledon. "No, we run like blazes!"

IV

PLEASE, ST. JOSEPH

THEY emerged at last, walking decorously, upon the Avenue des Boulevards and turned into the Terminus Cafe. This was not a hundred yards from the Place Rogier and Hambledon's hotel, this was more like home. Hambledon sank into a chair with a sigh of relief and ordered coffee for himself and a glass of wine for Letord.

"I thank you," said the detective. "We are well out of that adventure but still I am not happy."

"I am," said Tommy simply. "I am still alive."

"For that I rejoice sincerely, but apart from that what have we done? Nothing. Two men who have a minor part in this affair are in jail, which is pleasant but not helpful. Yanni is dead, which is neither helpful nor important. Burenne, my old friend Burenne, has run away and will no doubt come back——"

"If we went to the police and told them what we know about the murder of Yanni," said Hambledon, "they can arrest Burenne on our evidence."

"Presently, presently. At the moment I do not want the good Burenne arrested. I want him to lead me to his friends who deal in false currency. I have no shadow of right even to attempt to influence the actions of m'sieu', but if you could suppress for a time your English mania for abstract justice it would be a help. What," said Letord passionately, "what, is the necessity to avenge that spiv, Yanni, so urgent as to hamper such men as we in our investigations? We begin to discern the dim outline of a path which may take us somewhere near where we wish to go, and behold, there is the corpse of Yanni. If m'sieu' desires his justice at all cost, let him say so and I, Antoine Letord, will go home to my mother at Voutenay in the Department of Yonne and breed rabbits and pigeons. Racing pigeons, for they do at least get somewhere if it is only——"

"Stop, stop," said Hambledon. "Simmer down, come off the boil, extinguish yourself. What is all this? I don't care who Burenne bumps off so long as it isn't either of us. I only thought that if you had him under lock and key he might talk."

"Ah, no doubt he would, but how much does he know, that species? Take a parcel from Monsieur Brun in Brussels to Monsieur Blanc in Bruges, that is all, and where are we? Sucking our fingers round an empty mousetrap. I want Burenne to lead me to something he does not know himself, and then the Belgian police can have him for all I care. France has no use for him. I want some sort of proof," said Letord, banging the table.

"Have another *porto*," said Hambledon consolingly, and ordered it. "The question really is, where do we go from here? There are, of course, the girls."

"Girls? Girls? For the hours of leisure, by all means, but when on business I, Letord, am not——"

"Arrest yourself there, I was not suggesting dalliance. I meant the two girls who were in that house, didn't you see them? Old Papa sent them out before the fun started."

Letord's face cleared like an April day. "I apologize to m'sieu' a thousand times, I misunderstood the direction of his thoughts. There were two girls in that house, you say, and the old man sent them out? I did not see them, they must have come out while I was proceeding to that yard at the back. Do they live there? Then presumably they will return later."

"Only to find the police in possession," said Hambledon. "I don't know how they'll like that."

"You received not even the faintest hint of where they were to go?"

"You want jam on it," laughed Hambledon. "No. In my presence he merely told them to go out, but of course he was talking to them in the hall just before they started and I could not hear a word of that. Then he rang somebody on the telephone, as I told you; he may have been making an appointment for them. They may be anywhere."

"We can go back to the house and wait about till—— What is it?"

"Only a possibility that occurred to me. The parcel was in the house; when we looked for it it was not——"

"Did the girls take it?" said Letord, finishing Hambledon's sentence for him.

"Precisely."

Letord retired into a reverie so profound that he did not hear Hambledon ask him what he would drink next, so Tommy called up the waiter and ordered two filtered coffees. Coffee is said to be a brain stimulant and some such help was urgently needed, at the moment Hambledon felt that he had run out of ideas. He gave up trying to think for a few minutes and idly amused himself by watching their waiter. He was a neat little man with short black hair, very bright dark eyes and a small intelligent face. He was extraordinarily quick on his feet and deft in all his movements, he never seemed to tire and he was always smiling, a cheerful welcoming smile for every customer and every order. Hambledon thought he was like some friendly little animal, a squirrel perhaps, carrying things from place to place in quick short rushes. He would receive an order, smile, and dash up to the bar behind which the patron usually stood to serve the drinks; gather up glasses on a tray, scuttle back to the table with them and serve them with another smile. There was a sort of cash register on the bar which fascinated Hambledon; when the order was given the waiter would run to this piece of machinery. No cash went into it, the waiter merely punched levers till a label saying "6 Francs," or some such amount, rose at the back. Then he wound a handle like that of a musical-box at the side and a strip of paper emerged from a slit in the thing's fore-front. This was torn off, taken to the bar and stuck upon a wire spike —each waiter had his own spike—and the little man would scamper off again with a fresh load. Presumably there was a grand settlement of accounts when the cafe closed some time in the small hours.

Letord emerged from his retirement and said: "I have been thinking."

"So I noticed," said Hambledon. "Have some coffee. It might help."

"Tell me," said the detective, "what conclusion have you come to?"

"That our waiter is just like a well-trained squirrel. Look at him."

Letord looked at Hambledon instead and appealed to his Maker.

"Oh, very well," said Tommy, "if you think the moment has come to be serious, I'll do my best. The girls will probably not go to a house."

"For fear they should remember the address if anyone should ask at any time," agreed Letord. "I myself had considered that."

"They are probably walking up and down somewhere between certain specified limits until somebody comes along who is looking for two girls—description given— one of whom is carrying a brown-paper parcel. This coffee must be doing me good."

"But where in all the streets in Brussels——"

"Oh, not in any street in Brussels. Not in the quiet streets where two girls quarter-decking up and down for no obvious reason would attract notice. It would be somewhere where people always stroll up and down in the evenings, looking at the pretty lights, meeting their friends and occasionally dropping into a cafe."

"One of the boulevards, in short——"

"Like this one. I have been watching the passers-by hoping to see them. But I have not."

"So it isn't this boulevard," said Letord. He finished his coffee and rose to his feet. "We go and make a little promenade ourselves, eh? I am sorry, I remember you dislike walking."

"I don't mind walking," said Hambledon, signalling to the waiter. "It's running I can have too much of on a hot evening." He paid the man and they strolled out.

"You are right," said Letord, as one making a handsome concession. "That little man is like a squirrel."

"You have recovered," said Hambledon gravely. "I am glad."

They turned left out of the Terminus Cafe, took a brief glance round the Place Rogier and strolled on for a hundred yards. There were plenty of girls but not the two they sought, so they crossed the wide boulevard at the risk of their lives and strolled back.

"They are not here," said Letord, and steered Hambledon up the Rue Neuve as far as the Finistère.

"They are not here," said Hambledon, and conducted Letord into the Boulevard Adolphe Max. "I think we should have done ourselves just as much good if we'd gone into that church and burned a candle to St. Joseph."

"What happens then?"

"You say: 'Please, St. Joseph,' and leave off looking. Then, the first corner we turn, there are the two girls waiting for us."

Letord looked doubtfully at Hambledon, decided to take him seriously, and said that he himself was an agnostic.

"Ah, no doubt that would spoil it," said Tommy gravely. "Here is, at least, St. Michael on his pillar."

They walked round into the Boulevard Emile Jacqmain which brought them out eventually almost opposite to the Terminus Cafe from which they had started.

"Assuming," said Hambledon, "that they have not met their friend, handed over the parcel and gone home like good little girls an hour ago, let us turn left."

Letord sighed, and they plodded along the Boulevard d'Anvers past the shop where potatoes are so exquisitely fried; past fat girls and thin girls, tall girls and short girls, fair and dark girls, girls with stockings but mostly girls without, but never a sign of the tall haggard wench from the Rue Olive or her short solid friend who ironed.

At the end of the Boulevard they both sighed and crossed the road together as by pre-arrangement. They turned back towards the Place Rogier in silence; at the corner of the Rue du Théatre Hambledon halted suddenly and a large lady with a basket bumped into him from behind.

"A thousand pardons, madame," he said. "My clumsy stupidity."

"Enchanted, m'sieu'," she said cheerfully, and passed on.

"Our parcel," said Tommy in a low voice, "there he approaches. With the ladies, naturally. One in pink and the other in green." He walked up to the girls, swept off his hat and said that they were indeed well met. "And my parcel, permit me to relieve you of the burden."

Rather to his surprise the tall girl handed it over at once. "Glad to be done with it," she said heartily. "First it wasn't heavy and then it was and the more we walked the heavier it got. Brigitte carried it and I carried it—tell me, m'sieu', since it was you who were to have it why in the name of a little black dog could not the old Papa have given it to you at the house instead of constraining us to parade it round Brussels? Is it, then, a parcel which requires exercise?"

"I am not allowed to tell you in detail," said Hambledon mysteriously, "but it was not advisable for me to be seen leaving the house with it. I am sorry to have been so long——"

"For the past hour or more——"

55

"One hour and twenty minutes, Giselle," said the short girl.

"——have we been walking up and down this one block between these two streets——"

"I am desolated," said Hambledon, and meant it.

"Do you mean to tell me," said Letord, joining the group, "that if we had turned right coming out of that cafe we should have found these ladies in fifty yards instead of walking a mile and a half?"

"That is why I am desolated. Allow me—my friend Monsieur Letord—Mademoiselle Giselle, Mademoiselle Brigitte." He paused for the conventional murmurs of "*Enchantee m'sieu'*," and added: "You must be as exhausted as we. Permit me to suggest a little refreshment."

He led the party into the Terminus, explaining that he liked the waiter, and ordered wine for the girls and beer for Letord and himself. They sat at one of the small tables on the pavement; Hambledon put down the parcel on an empty chair between himself and Letord, and relaxed comfortably.

"Your good Papa," he began.

"Not my Papa," said Giselle instantly, "nor Brigitte's. We only lodge there, you understand. We just call him Papa. I suppose he didn't tell you exactly where to find us, just like him, isn't it, Brigitte? He's not a bad old thing really, but he's terribly silly sometimes. I think he's getting worse, and so does Brigitte. Look at the way he told us to go out tonight, just because he wanted to talk to you. We could have sat up in our rooms, couldn't we? I've got a nice room. No, we must go out, and lugging that miserable parcel, too; anyone would think we were the sort who listened at keyholes and I've never done such a thing in my life, nor has Brigitte, have you, Brigitte? I think he's been getting more tiresome lately—your health, m'sieu', and thank you—anyone would think he paid us to work for him, whereas we pay him rent for our rooms and a good rent too, don't we, Brigitte? If he goes on like this I don't think I'll stop there much longer, being ordered about like a servant. I don't know what he's thinking of. I think I'll have a good talk with him when we go back tonight, you'll back me up, won't you, Brigitte? I shall tell him——"

"I don't think you'll have to," said Hambledon.

"What?"

"Since he's not your Papa I don't mind telling you. He has been arrested by the police."

"Arrested! Brigitte, do you hear that? Arrested——"

"I am not altogether surprised," said Brigitte, speaking for the first time.

"Nor am I. I have thought there was something funny going on for some time past, I have honest, I'm not just saying that because of what happened tonight."

"Tell me," said Hambledon, "what has happened which you think is funny."

"Oh, people coming to the house, and messages on the telephone, and sometimes the front parlour's all locked up and sometimes it isn't, and your head bitten off if you ask why."

"What sort of people?"

"Generally we don't see them, they're taken into the front room or we're chased off upstairs. All I know is, some people bring parcels and some fetch them. Well, you know all about that, don't you, since this parcel is for you? Oh! Are the police after you, too?"

"No, Mademoiselle Giselle, happily they are not. I know about this parcel, yes, it's the others I am curious about."

"I see. This one's different."

"Precisely, mademoiselle. About these people who come to the house. Can it really be that you have never seen any of them?"

"The man with the Citroën," said Brigitte.

Giselle nodded. "Him we do know though he takes no notice of us but to grin and say the day is fine. He brings parcels in his old Citroën and carries them in just like a laundry boy bringing home the washing. He is not interested in girls, that one."

"He is, perhaps, happily married," said Letord. "Does he wear a wedding ring?"

"No, m'sieu', but he might be married for all that. He looks married, I think. Brigitte, does Maurice look married?"

"What is it," asked Brigitte darkly, "this married look?"

Hambledon laughed and asked what Maurice did look like, and Giselle described him very clearly. A man of the middle class, a shopkeeper perhaps, not a *restaurateur*, he had not those manners. He was still young, about thirty, brown hair, grey eyes, about five feet eight inches tall. He had a square face broad across the cheek-bones—Giselle gestured—and a square jaw. He was sunburnt, but then he never wore a hat. Brigitte interposed to say he had nice hands and Giselle said Brigitte was mad about hands, she had a theory about them. Letord averted the theory by asking whether Maurice's ears stuck out and was told they did not. He wore rather shabby clothes, good clothes but they had been worn a lot. "I expect he buys them second-hand from somebody's valet," said Giselle. The car was very shabby and she had asked him one day why he didn't enliven it with a little paint. He laughed and said perhaps he would some day when he could afford it.

Letord turned to Hambledon and, making a great effort, spoke in English. "I t'ink dis packet more safer ellesvair, no?'"

"Absolutely," agreed Hambledon, and reverted to French. "If the ladies will excuse me a moment—a short five minutes—I will put this parcel in a place of safety and return. After that we might do something amusing, a cinema possibly——"

"Oh, please! There is 'The Mysterious Monsieur Sylvain' at the Crosly-Nord——"

"Very well. Letord will entertain you till I return and then we will go and interview the mysterious gentleman."

Hambledon went back to his own room at the Albert and was just about to drop the parcel in a drawer when his room telephone rang. It was Letord speaking.

"I catch you, my friend, it is well. There is a man who keeps on passing and looking *in*; he looks at the girls."

"Tell me," said Hambledon solemnly, "why are all the bad men of Europe pursuing Monsieur Letord? Surely that is all the wrong way round. First Burenne and now—what did you say?"

Letord said it again and Hambledon held the receiver a little away from his ear. It was more comfortable like that.

"Listen," said Tommy. "Speaking seriously, I don't think I like this much, on account of those girls. If he is after that parcel he might take it out of them for parting with it. I think I'll make up another parcel and bring it back to the Terminus. He can then amuse himself trying to get it away from us. Does he know you?"

"Not to my knowledge but I would not rely upon it."

"Umph. Well, I'll bring back a parcel and make it clear that I've got it. That ought to distract his attention from Brigitte and Giselle. Is she still talking?"

Letord gave it as his opinion that Giselle ought to hire herself out to scare birds and rang off. Hambledon tore open the parcel, dropped bundles of assorted currency into his bottom drawer and rolled up a jacket and two pairs of flannel trousers in their place. He tucked the resultant parcel under his arm and returned to the Terminus. Giselle, now well into her third glass of port, was still talking.

"There was one new one who came the other day," she said. "He had nothing in his hands when he came so I suppose he took something away. I do not know. I did but open the door to him, I was expecting a friend. I did not like that one, he was French, one of your apaches, m'sieu' Letord. But, m'sieu'! You still have your parcel after all? You cannot bear to be parted from your so precious one! I am jealous, me!"

"Silly," said Brigitte, upon whom port had no effect. "It isn't the same, it's tied up differently."

"Mademoiselle," said Hambledon, "your bright eyes are very observant."

Letord made another effort in English. "'E is now there, in the road."

"Then he'll get run over," said Tommy cheerfully, "and all's well." He lifted his glass of beer and looked casually over the rim of it. There was an island down the middle of the road against which the trams stopped; on the edge of this a young man was standing looking across at the cafe. Hambledon put his parcel on the table close against his chest and leaned his elbow on it; the young man was plainly interested but at that moment a rush of traffic passed in front of him.

"There will be a snatch in a minute," said Hambledon in slow English under cover of Giselle's opinion of Clark Gable. "I think I'll take the parcel to the patron at the bar at the back. We are too easy, in front here. Then your friend will have to come right in if he wants to get it."

Letord nodded. "Wait till 'e can see plain." He paused a moment till there was a gap in the traffic. " 'E looks. 'E comes across. Now."

Hambledon rose to his feet, picked up his parcel and walked deliberately up the central gangway between the tables on the floor of the restaurant. The bar was a short counter on the right. Behind the main floor of the cafe four steps led up to a further space where meals were served. There was an ornate arch over the steps with a spiral pillar, heavily gilt, on either side; the diners could look down from their elevation upon the mere drinkers below. At the back of the dining-room, stairs in the corner led down to a telephone room and toilets in the basement.

Hambledon went up to the bar and asked the proprietor if he would be so good as to keep this parcel for a short time, it was an inconvenience on a small table. The proprietor agreed at once and put the parcel up on one of his shelves at the back of the bar; Tommy returned to his seat and resumed his beer.

The young man had returned to the street refuge and appeared to be disconcerted. He shifted irresolutely about and strolled a few steps up and down. He stopped, drew a wallet from his pocket and looked at something which he took out of it.

"Reading the directions?" murmured Tommy.

The man put his wallet back in his pocket and walked away, crossing the road diagonally in the direction of the Place Rogier. Hambledon and Letord waited for some minutes but he did not reappear.

" 'E 'as gone," said Letord. " 'E 'as give up."

"Perhaps it's as well," said Tommy Hambledon. "I don't really enjoy violence."

V

STEWPAN

HAMBLEDON relaxed in his chair, suppressed a yawn and glanced at his watch which said that the time was a quarter to midnight; early indeed for Brussels which never goes to bed until the small hours but late enough for him upon this occasion. So much had happened since he started from his hotel at six that evening with the intention of catching a train to Antwerp that he found it hard to believe that this was still the same day. If only they could shed these two excellent girls—better escort them home to make sure they arrived there safely—he could return to the Albert Premier and retire to bed. Such a comfortable bed. He yawned irrepressibly this time and caught Letord's eye, the detective nodded. Giselle was still chattering, Brigitte's comments were fewer and increasingly pointed, the restaurant was full of people and babble and the waiters dashed feverishly about, intoning their orders to the patron who ceaselessly filled glasses, set them down and filled more. Hambledon framed an excuse for breaking up the party and moved forward on his chair to speak.

There came a sudden hush as startling as an explosion of sound, it began at the back of the room and travelled forward like a wave. Giselle noticed it and broke off with a suppressed squeal, Hambledon looked round sharply.

At the foot of the four steps to the dining-room stood the young man who had been standing on the tram refuge. His face was white and dark eyes blazed under the peak of his cloth cap. He was pointing a revolver at the proprietor who was standing in front of the bar with his hands up. Behind the bar the squirrel-like waiter stood frozen in the act of setting down a tray and for a moment nobody moved. The scene was like some unexpected tableau, even the lights seemed brighter just in that spot.

Hambledon found himself whispering to the waiter with the tray: "Throw it, man! Throw it!" Behind him Giselle was whimpering that it was he, the French apache who had been to their house. The gangster's lips moved; though his words were inaudible across the room the tableau came to life. The proprietor shifted sideways a little and the waiter behind the bar set down his tray. He turned and lifted Hambledon's parcel down from the shelf, stepped smartly forward and handed it to the gangster with a quick bow and a smile as for any other order in the day's work.

The parcel was large and no doubt the young man expected to find it heavy. He snatched it with both hands, dropping his gun as he did so, and turned to run up the steps and out through the basement by the way he had come in, but the waiter was too quick for him. With a curious dancing step he dodged round the bar, snatched up the revolver and fired upwards at the back of the young man's head. He dropped the parcel, staggered upon the top step and fell with a crash between the tables.

Instantly the place was in an uproar. Women screamed; people leapt from their seats, recoiling against the walls, and Madame the proprietress at the table opposite the bar

fainted where she sat and swept a large bowl of mussels—
la specialité de la maison—off the table. It smashed on the
floor and the mussels scattered in all directions and
cracked under people's feet. Letord said: "I fetch police,"
and dashed out into the road. Almost at the same moment
another man jumped the low railings in front of the cafe,
ran forward and dived headfirst into the milling crowd
round the body. He reappeared at once carrying the
parcel and came running down the aisle between the
tables; Hambledon dodged out to intercept him but
changed his mind at the sight of a knife in the man's hand.
No sensible Englishman risks his life for a sports jacket
and two pairs of flannel bags.

Giselle stared, gasped, clutched Hambledon by the arm
and hissed: "Maurice! That was Maurice! He has our
parcel!"

"Oh, really," said Hambledon, very interested. "The
man who drives the old Citroën, eh? So that's Maurice.
Arrived very promptly, didn't he?"

"But our parcel——"

Hambledon caught the eye of Brigitte who merely
looked faintly amused.

"Do you agree, Brigitte, that that was Maurice?"

"Without a doubt."

"Thank you. Well, he's got the parcel and as he can
probably run a lot faster than I can I think he'll have to keep
it for the present. At least we know who took it, which is
always a help."

Letord returned with a large man in the blue uniform
and white helmet of the Belgian Police. The Frenchman
forced a way through the press, exclaiming loudly that
he was a doctor and would examine the man if the police-

man would have the goodness to hold the crowd back. Hambledon stayed where he was, merely standing upon a chair to watch with admiration the way Letord rolled the body over to feel for heart-beats. The detective straightened up again, turned to the police agent, and said: "This man is not dead at all. He is not going to die, at least, not of this. The bullet did but graze the skull and stun him."

"In that case," said the policeman, "perhaps m'sieu' the patron has a store-room with a lock on it where this man can be stowed until the police can come with a conveyance to remove him."

"But, certainly," said the proprietor. "Below, in the basement. Alphonse, Jules, Ercule, convey this bandit down the stairs and lock him in number two. Here is the key. Victor, a wet mop for this floor."

Waiters rushed to obey and the unconscious man was hustled down the stairs with more zeal than tenderness. The policeman expressed a wish to use the telephone and was also directed down to the basement. The proprietor rushed to attend to his wife who was showing signs of returning animation among the mussels, the clients became at once calmer and a lot more talkative and Letord slipped quietly away to join Hambledon and the girls. Giselle was sobbing with excitement, hysteria and port; Brigitte, white in the face but entirely composed, was powdering her nose with the help of a hand-bag mirror.

"Get out of here," said Letord under his breath. "Come on." He lifted Giselle to her feet, shook her and practically carried her into the street; Hambledon, who was developing a comparative affection for the imperturbable Brigitte, slipped his hand through her arm and followed. Round the corner in the Place Rogier Letord signalled a taxi and levered Giselle into it, Brigitte followed sedately. Hambledon bowed over her hand and thanked her for a pleasant evening, adding: "Permit me to have the privilege of paying for the taxi." He closed her fingers over some notes while Letord gave the Rue Olive address to the driver, and slammed the door. The taxi drove away with Giselle waving and Brigitte busy examining what she held in her hand.

"They will find the house empty when they get back," said Hambledon. "Unless the police are still there."

"Brigitte will manage," said Letord.

"And if the police are not there," continued Hambledon, "how will they get in?"

"Brigitte will manage. Through the window. How much did you give her?"

"Two hundred francs. I thought she'd earned it."

"And they say England is poor," said Letord, leading the way across the square.

"It's only about twenty-two and sixpence in our money. Not too much as a reward for not talking all the evening."

"Oh boy," said Letord carefully, "you 'ave something got there." After a moment's thought he added: "I vill say."

They completed their passage to the Albert Premier in silence.

Up in Hambledon's bedroom with the door locked and a chair tilted under the handle as an extra precaution, they examined the bundles of notes which had been in the parcel. They were Belgian notes of fifty and hundred franc denominations and there were several hundred of them. Hambledon looked at the display with something like awe; previously he had only seen samples, not the accumulated results of mass-production.

"And this is only one parcel out of many," he said thoughtfully. "I suppose they are all forgeries?"

Letord, who was examining with a magnifying-glass notes picked out at random, merely nodded.

"I had not quite realized," went on Hambledon, "the scale of these operations. If Old Papa is only one distributing centre in Belgium and there are many others doing as well as he, it won't be long before the Belgian currency is doubled and then what happens?"

"Inflation, they tell me, I am no financier. What the Government can do in such a case is to call in all the present currency and issue a new one quite different in appearance. They have done so once already since the War ended, they will not wish to do so again so soon."

"Besides, imagine the queues of people waiting while cashiers scrutinize every note with a magnifying-glass——"

"Most of which notes," said Letord sadly, "please remember, will have been quite honestly obtained by the poor folk who hand them in. When they are told that perhaps half of their money is worthless and cannot be replaced, what happens?"

"Riots, I imagine."

"Oh, riots," said the Frenchman, waving away riots. "These commotions, they happen. No, it is the little private miseries, the individual despairs, the personal disappointments, the tears shed in little lonely rooms; they haunt me, m'sieu', they haunt me. These people who deal in these," said Letord, picking up one of the bundles of notes and hurling it to the floor, "guillotining is too good for them. They should be strangled, they should be drowned like the rats they are." He stopped abruptly and Hambledon noticed with sympathy that his eyes were full of tears. "Forgive me, m'sieu', for my emotion, but the same thing is happening in France. Then the suicide rate will begin to rise and we of the police, we drag them out of rivers or clean up after them when they blow out their brains or cut their throats——"

"Have a cigarette," said Hambledon, and patted him on the shoulder.

"I thank m'sieu'."

"And now tell me, what did you get out of that fellow's pocket?"

Letord's strained expression relaxed. "You did not see me do it, no? Not even when you stand on your chair?"

"Oh Lord, no. I did rather wonder that nobody else thought it funny to feel a man's heart when his pulse is so much more convenient."

"It is the air of authority," said Letord simply. "I have it by nature and assiduous practice." He felt in his pocket. "I took his wallet, of course, here it is."

He put on his gloves and turned out the contents of the wallet. "Identity papers and passport, forged I expect. What is this?"

A photograph slid out from the pages of the passport, a glossy print of a girl's face, fair-haired and snub-nosed with lips a little parted. On the corner of the photograph was a recent thumb-print well defined on the glazed surface.

"This, I suppose, was what he was looking at on the street refuge just before he walked away," said Hambledon. "You remember."

"Perfectly. You made the snatch too difficult, so he screws himself up to the attack. He is nervous, his hand is damp. It is a lovely print." Letord turned the photograph over. "And here are prints of two fingers on the back. In Paris they will tell us all about him; the photographer, whose rubber stamp is on the back, will inform us about the girl. It marches, my friend, slowly, but it marches."

"Splendid," said Hambledon, and yawned suddenly.

"You are fatigued," said Letord sympathetically. "I recommend the bed. Tomorrow m'sieu' will be as a lion restored."

"What about the Belgian police? This evidence is really theirs, isn't it?"

"Assuredly. I am going now to the City Police headquarters where one will summon for me the Chief of Police. Thus the affair will be regularised. I will take also these bundles of forged notes. I wish m'sieu' the sleep of the righteous," said Letord, opening the door. "Good night and a thousand thanks. I will see m'sieu' in the morning."

He went away and Hambledon locked the door after him. Bed was certainly the best idea. Tommy began removing his clothes, the trouser-hanger, where was it? Hang the trouser-hanger, the garment would do just as well over the towel-rail for one night. At this point the telephone rang, he regarded it with bitter distaste and let it ring in the hope that it would stop. It persevered, he sighed and lifted the receiver.

The hotel clerk said that he was desolated to disturb m'sieu' but a lady wished to speak to him and it was urgent, urgent! At least, the clerk believed that it was he with whom the lady wished to speak, she did not know his name but there was a description which appeared to fit m'sieu' better than any other of their patrons.

Hambledon said that he had talked with ladies quite sufficiently for one evening and the clerk had better swivel her on to somebody else.

The clerk made comprehending noises but added that the lady said it was a matter of life and death.

Hambledon said in a frigid tone that they always said that and asked as an afterthought what her name was.

"Brigitte, she says."

"Put her through," said Tommy in a resigned voice.

Brigitte said that she wanted m'sieu' to come to the Rue Olive at once, at once, something had happened.

"What has happened, precisely?"

"Maurice is here."

"Maurice?"

"He is in the coal-hole."

"Hiding?" asked Tommy.

"No, m'sieu'. Locked in. He threatened us with a gun."

"Oh. Very well. I will come at once."

Hambledon threw his clothes on again and took a taxi to the Rue Olive; as it stopped the door opened and Giselle looked out. Hambledon paid off the taxi-driver and went in.

"Now then——"

"Oh, m'sieu', we arrive here and climb in through the kitchen window with the broken catch. So we have supper together and Brigitte is just about to make coffee when there is a knock at the front door and there was Maurice. He said he had got the wrong parcel and we told him not to be silly, it was the same parcel all the time."

"You told him that, did you, Giselle?"

"But certainly. You know Brigitte, if you wait for an answer from that one you will await also Michaelmas. I told him what took place and he did not believe me. He said this parcel was full of clothes and I said well, what ought it to have in it? He would not tell me. He was very angry."

"I don't know that I blame him," said Hambledon thoughtfully.

"He called us the most dreadful names, m'sieu', and then he searched the house, didn't he, Brigitte? Pulled out drawers and flung them to the floor and threw things out of cupboards all the time swearing most dreadfully. Then he came back into the kitchen and said if we did not tell him truthfully where the other parcel was he would shoot us. He got out his gun and said we had taken the parcel and given it to one of our boy-friends and when I said that what I'd told him before was perfectly true he pointed the gun at me and said if I did not speak before he had counted ten he would shoot. So he began to count; one, two, three—and then Brigitte stepped back and hit him on the head with the stewpan."

"Stewpan?"

"This one," said Brigitte, and displayed it. It was a large and heavy iron pan, shallow, but nearly a foot across, with a long handle. It must have weighed six or seven pounds.

"Good gracious," said Hambledon, making as it were approach shots with it. "Is he dead?"

"Oh no, m'sieu'. He did but fall down——"

"I should darn well think so," said Hambledon.

"So we dragged him along between us, pushed him into the coal-hole——"

"He was snoring," said Brigitte.

"——and locked the door. Then we did not know what it was wise to do so we rang you up, at least, Brigitte did."

"Yes. On the whole it was probably wise. Well, I suppose I'd better see him."

"His gun, m'sieu'," said Brigitte, indicating it with one foot since it was still lying on the floor where Maurice dropped it when he encountered the stewpan.

"We did not like to touch it, m'sieu'," said Giselle. "We do not understand these things, not even Brigitte, and it might have gone off and shot us."

"I wonder it didn't when you pipped him with the pan," said Hambledon, picking up the revolver.

"He did look so funny!" said Giselle with a peal of laughter. "First his eyes close, then he smiles as one who has the happy dream, then he drops his gun and then at last his knees bend and he goes down—thud! Didn't he, Brigitte?"

"This is a clumsy great thing," said Hambledon. "I think I'll——"

"It is big, isn't it, m'sieu'? When he pointed it at me and I could see right down the ugly mouth of it it got bigger and bigger—it did, truly, m'sieu'!"

"I daresay. Well, I think we'll put this out of sight somewhere for the present."

"I thought you might want it," said Brigitte, putting it away in a dresser drawer.

"Thank you, but I've got one of my own, I prefer it."

"Oh, m'sieu', I didn't know you were a gun-man!"

"You didn't, Giselle, did you? Well now, where's this coal-hole of yours?"

Brigitte conducted him through a door at the far end of the kitchen and indicated a locked door in the passage behind. "Listen," she said. A heavy intermittent noise came from within. "He sleeps," said Brigitte, and smiled like an angel. Hambledon was quite startled, he found time to reflect that he had never seen Brigitte smile before. A queer girl. He unlocked the door and opened it.

Inside was a small space about three feet wide by five feet long; the unconscious man was huddled up on the floor in an extremely uncomfortable position made worse by a quantity of round briquettes—like black cricket-balls—which covered the floor.

"You seem to have made a job of it, certainly," said Hambledon. "I think we'd better get him out. I want to talk to him. If I lift his shoulders could you girls take a leg each?"

"Pull him out," said Brigitte. She took hold of both ankles and heaved and Maurice came out sliding; the loose briquettes beneath him acting upon the roller principle known to the prehistoric builders of Stonehenge. Giselle, with a squeak of joy, seized one ankle and the two girls towed Maurice along the passage into the kitchen with his head bumping behind him.

"There," said Brigitte, and looked at Hambledon for further instructions.

"If I poured a bucket of water over him," said Tommy Hambledon, "I should make a mess of your nice clean floor."

Brigitte seized the stewpan, lifted Maurice's head by the hair and put the pan underneath, after which she filled a jug with cold water and poured a steady stream upon his forehead.

"You know," said Hambledon thoughtfully, "don't imagine I don't like you, because I do, but if I were ill I don't think I'd want you to nurse me. Just a moment, it may save an argument if I go through his pockets before he wakes up."

His pockets yielded little of interest. A wallet containing a few franc notes both Belgian and French, the return half of a railway ticket to Paris, and a letter without envelope beginning: "My dear Maurice" and signed Colette. The address at the head of the letter was a street in Paris. Tommy put the wallet in his own pocket for further examination and proceeded. Two keys on a ring; some loose coins; a cigarette lighter and a packet of Davros cigarettes and a handkerchief, unmarked. In a leather sheath attached to his trouser-band at the hip, the wicked-looking double-edged knife he had produced at the cafe.

"Not much here," said Tommy, and nodded to Brigitte standing with the jug poised for further action. "Carry on."

She obeyed and Maurice began to respond. He left off snoring and groaned instead, rolled about and tried to open his eyes. The light, shining straight into them from the unshaded electric bulb, was evidently painful for he shut them again and put his hands over them muttering something about his head. Then the rim of the stewpan under the back of his neck began to make itself felt; he fumbled behind his head, saying thickly: "What the devil's this?" and tried to roll off it.

"Sit up!" said Hambledon peremptorily. "Come away, Brigitte." Brigitte did, bringing her stewpan with her, and looked with interest at the Lüger automatic in

Hambledon's hand. Maurice sat up, blinking and supporting himself with one hand on the floor. He ran the other over his head and winced when he came to an area above his right ear.

"That will teach you to threaten girls with guns," said Giselle cheerfully.

Maurice opened his eyes, looked at her and blinked, then at Brigitte and flinched, and finally at Hambledon, gun in hand, standing between the two girls like the central plume in the Prince of Wales' Feathers.

"Who are you?" asked Maurice indistinctly.

"No concern of yours. You will answer my questions. Where do you live?"

Maurice's jaw came forward and he said: "Find out."

"Very well. What did you come here for?"

Maurice did not answer.

"Why did you come here tonight?"

"Why not?"

"Very well," said Hambledon again. "If you won't talk to me you can talk to somebody else, that's all. It doesn't really matter. Brigitte, do you see how I am holding this gun? That bit there is called the trigger and if you pull on it with your finger the gun will go off and probably kill somebody. Stand quite still with your finger just resting—no more—on the trigger and point the gun at Maurice. No, not his head, he might duck suddenly and you might miss. Point it right in the middle of his pull-over, that's right. Hold it steadily and don't move till I come back. I am going to phone for the police. Maurice, if I were you I wouldn't try any funny business."

Maurice didn't.

VI

HANDCUFFS FOR HAMBLEDON

THE police arrived and took Maurice into custody on a charge of breaking into number 208 Rue Olive and menacing with a loaded revolver the two young women who lived there. Giselle told the story; Brigitte briefly corroborated, producing Maurice's revolver as evidence: Maurice stood against the wall with water still dripping from his hair and a policeman attending closely upon him, and Hambledon leaned against the dresser placidly waiting to answer such questions as might lawfully be addressed to him. He was beginning to feel sleepy again.

The senior of the two police officers sat at the table and took down notes. When it came to Hambledon's turn the sergeant leaned back in his chair and looked the Englishman up and down.

"And what exactly, m'sieu', was your part in this little affair?"

Hambledon explained that the ladies, being alarmed by the intrusion of this brigand, had called upon him for assistance and advice.

"Very natural, certainly. Though it appears to me that the ladies dealt with the brigand with resolution and despatch before your arrival, if I have their story correctly.

77

Ladies who can stun a man with a stewpan and throw him into a coal-cellar might, one imagines, have had the strength to ring up the police direct without asking assistance from anyone?"

Hambledon blinked and said that it was not for him to analyse the motives of ladies. The affair had been as he had described. Reaction, possibly, had set in. The after-effects of violence and alarm.

The sergeant nodded thoughtfully and said that one had, in fact, heard of cases like that. "What I want to know," he added sharply, "is, which of you went through his pockets?" He indicated the small heap of Maurice's possessions on the end of the table.

"I did," said Hambledon. "He might have had other arms besides that revolver. He had. That knife."

"Precisely. It is odd, however, that there is no money, no papers and not even a wallet."

"I've got his wallet," said Tommy, and produced it. "I put it in my pocket for safety."

"For safety," repeated the sergeant. "Not from habit?"

"Dammit, do you take me for a pickpocket?"

"I do not know. You have given me a name and an address in England, how do I know that they are genuine?" Tommy gave him a good mark for that one, the name on his papers was not Hambledon. "Listen, m'sieu'. You appear to me to be a gentleman of culture and established position and if I do wrong my superiors will tell me. But, earlier this evening, two men were arrested in this street and one of them owns this house. You were seen walking away from this neighbourhood at that time, you and another man, I met you myself as I was coming here. Later, there is a fracas in a cafe in the Avenue des Boulevards. I do not suggest that you had any part in it, but when I arrive there—having been notified that there was a little trouble—you are coming out with these two ladies. There is again trouble in this house; I come and once more behold m'sieu'. I have no wish to be offensive but I say to myself that m'sieu' has at least been a little unlucky. I am taking you to the police station for further enquiries."

Hambledon gave in at once; the man was not only within his rights but would be greatly to blame if he acted otherwise. At the same time there remained the empty bed in the Albert Premier and Tommy's yearning for it amounted to an ache. There was just one more expedient which was worth trying.

"Your suspicions are natural," he said. "All the same—may I write something down? It is for your private eye alone."

"You may write briefly," said the sergeant. Hambledon looked round for paper of some kind, even as he did so Brigitte handed him a block of cheap ruled paper and a pencil.

"What a secretary you'd make," said Tommy, and wrote a message for the sergeant. "I am Thomas Elphinstone Hambledon of British Intelligence visiting Belgium on official business. Your Chief of Police knows me personally." He detached the sheet and handed it to the sergeant who read it through, rose, and bowed politely.

"I am honoured by your confidence, m'sieu'. Nevertheless, a man of m'sieu's experience must be well aware that this proves nothing and that it does not relieve me from the unpleasant necessity of checking m'sieu's statements. I regret I must still ask you to accompany me to the police station."

"Oh, very well," said Hambledon in a resigned voice. "I only wanted to go to bed, it doesn't really matter."

"And one other liberty my duty compels me to take," continued the sergeant. "M'sieu' sees that I am short-handed and one of us must drive the car. It follows that I must, with regret, handcuff m'sieu' to this other prisoner here. It is, happily, but a short distance to the police station where matters can be regularised by my superior officers."

"It also follows," began Hambledon angrily, "that I have been talking to you for twenty minutes without producing the slightest effect——"

"A police officer upon whom talking produced the effect of neglecting his duty would not last long in Belgium, m'sieu'."

Hambledon laughed suddenly. "You are right, of course. Produce your manacles." The sergeant did so and in the course of putting the handcuff round Tommy's wrist, brushed against his coat pocket and neatly removed the Lüger. Hambledon laughed again, it seemed the only thing to do. The room seemed curiously quiet, there was something missing as when a clock ceases to tick. Of course, the missing sound was the voice of Giselle. Sunk in the only armchair the room contained, she was peacefully asleep. Hambledon, now handcuffed to Maurice, glanced at Brigitte.

"Don't worry," she said, "I'll manage."

"I'm sure you will——"

"But as for m'sieu'——"

"It is my turn to say 'don't worry'. This is a misunderstanding. I will see you tomorrow."

"But——" said Brigitte again.

"All right," said Hambledon. "If I ring you up in half an hour's time to tell you I am free, will you believe me?"

"Certainly, m'sieu'."

"Very well, I'll do that."

"Forward," said the sergeant, and conducted his captives from the house to the car.

At Brussels' principal police station Hambledon was led in accompanied inevitably by Maurice. They walked into the Charge-room by one door exactly as the Chief of Police, with Letord, entered by another. Hambledon beamed upon them and said it was a pleasant evening, was it not? Less tiring, with the onset of night's coolness.

"But you are handcuffed!" said the Chief of Police, and sprang forward. "Who did this? Unlock these——"

"Don't get annoyed, please," said Hambledon. "Believe me, I am not. Your sergeant had good reason to think my conduct suspicious and took all necessary precautions. In my opinion, if I may be permitted to express it, he was perfectly justified."

The Chief said that it was extremely generous of Hambledon to say so, but there was such a thing as lack of tact and excess of zeal.

"Not at all," said Tommy stoutly. "I have been arrested many times in different countries upon various pretexts, but never with such delicate politeness as I met tonight. Belgium for courtesy, without a doubt."

The Chief of Police appeared sufficiently calmed to enquire who Maurice was, and Hambledon, released from his fetters, strolled across to the French detective.

"I thought m'sieu' was in bed and asleep an hour ago," said Letord.

"I should have missed something comic if I had been. I'll tell you later. In the meantime that's Maurice, the Man With The Citroën."

"Being charged with breaking and entering and menacing somebody with a revolver?"

"Certainly. Very naturally, too, we ought to have foreseen it. He opened his parcel and found my flannel bags instead of what he expected. Enough to annoy anybody, you must admit that. He went up to the Rue Olive to ask for an explanation. Brigitte managed him." The Chief of Police had completed his enquiries into what appeared to him to be a case of the utmost triviality and came towards Hambledon who said in a low voice that he had information of considerable importance. The Chief led the way into his office and shut the door.

"That man," said Hambledon, "is one of the distributors of forged currency. He runs round in an old Citroën handing out parcels. No doubt Letord has told you all the rest. You have also Old Papa in custody, have you not? I am sorry to be so informal but I don't know these people's names." He went on to give an account of Maurice's misadventures in the Rue Olive.

"This Maurice is stupid," said Letord thoughtfully. "He should have shot Brigitte."

Hambledon scowled suddenly and the Chief of Police said that he thought, from what he had heard, that both those young women would be safer in some other city. "After, of course, they have given evidence—wait a minute. It is necessary to consider how much of this evidence it is advisable to make public."

"If you're thinking of coaching the girl Giselle in exactly how much she is to say and where she is to stop, I pity you," said Letord.

"One of our gas-jets?" said the Chief. "Just so. The affair requires consideration."

"In the meantime," said Hambledon, "there is in Maurice's wallet a letter from a woman in Paris."

"Oh, is there?" said the Chief. He rang a bell and ordered the wallet to be brought to him. He opened the letter and read it aloud.

My dear Maurice,

Forgive me that I write to you in some agitation. I have to thank you for returning to me the money which I lent you when last we met, but I am sorry to tell you that there was trouble over some of the notes. I changed several of them in shops without difficulty, but when I went to deposit the remainder at my bank they refused to accept them, saying that they were forgeries. I do not believe for a moment, dear Maurice, that you would have sent them to me if you had known them to be false, I merely tell you this to warn you that some one of your sources of supply is unreliable.

I must admit that this little episode has made me anxious for your welfare. It is well known that there are dishonest and unpatriotic organizations engaged in making and distributing forged notes, it is my fear that you may have become involved, however unwittingly, with agents of such an organization. Dear Maurice, do be careful, these men are cunning and ruthless, if once they succeed in involving you in their wicked proceedings the only outcome must be disgrace or death. Forgive me if I appear importunate, you know that your interests are very close to my heart. Write, please write to me at once and assure me that you have taken steps to find the source of these forgeries and that you will avoid it in the future as you would some foul pestilence. They will drag you down, they will ruin you. Save yourself, Maurice, I beg.

I am, yours in all friendship,
Colette.

"When was this dated?" asked Hambledon.

"Ten days ago."

"Oh. I think an interview with the lady might be helpful, don't you, Letord? What a dirty dog this Maurice is, he borrows money from a girl-friend and pays her back in forged notes."

"You notice," said Letord, "that although she wraps it up in layers of tact, she is pretty sure he is mixed up in it."

"She believes him capable of it, anyway," said the Belgian.

"Yes, that is very plain. Now, I think we go to Paris by the first available train. I am sure that M. Hambledon can be trusted to make the most of the lady. As for me, I wish to go to Paris to make enquiries about the other young man at whom the waiter fired in the Terminus cafe tonight. The fingerprints upon that photograph will almost certainly be in our records and then we shall at least know who he is. Besides, there is the girl of the photograph."

"The young man himself," said Tommy, "I suppose he is not yet well enough to talk?"

"I forgot, you do not know. He is gone, that one. He

was locked in a store-room at the Terminus till the police ambulance should come; when they do arrive he is not there."

"Rescued?"

"Undoubtedly. There is a staircase down from the street to that basement, very inconspicuous, a service entrance. That was the way he entered, naturally, and no doubt his friends waited outside to see what happened. They simply walked in and took him away again."

"Tiresome," said Hambledon. "Never mind, I expect he'll turn up somewhere. At least you know what he looks like which is always so helpful. We go to Paris tomorrow, Letord, do we?"

The detective looked at his watch and said that, speaking correctly, it was today since the hour was already two in the morning, and that the train leaving Brussels at five minutes past four in the afternoon would be quite soon enough. Also there were Pullman cars on that train in which it was possible to book a seat and avoid the violent struggle which was otherwise necessary to get on a train at all. No doubt Hambledon, being English, had been trained in the Rugby football scrum exertions since his childhood; but for himself, said Letord, he had neither the weight nor the inclination for these more exhausting forms of exercise. In England, no doubt, to enter the train was considered a wholesome and hearty masculine sport.

Hambledon yawned, apologized, and said not at all, the English stood in queues. First come, first served.

"But when the train comes in? Do the people not rush together then?"

"Not even then."

"Formidable," said Letord.

Hambledon said that if nobody wanted him any more that evening he would rather like to go to bed. The police sympathised and he returned to his hotel. A nice hotel, the lift worked all night, he would not even have to walk up the stairs. He nodded to the night porter, who was in the act of answering the telephone, and walked along to the lift; before he reached it he was stopped by cries of "M'sieu'! M'sieu'!" from the porter.

"What is it?"

A lady urgently desired to speak with him on the telephone. "The same lady as before," said the porter, nobly suppressing a smile.

"Oh gosh," said Hambledon, who had completely forgotten his promise to ring up Brigitte. "All right, I'll speak to her. Hullo? That you, Brigitte? Sorry I couldn't ring up before but I've only this moment come in. Everything's all right and your friend with the bump on his head is safely locked up, so now you can go peacefully to sleep. What's that? Burgled? Oh, not again, surely. Are you all right? That's good. Did he take anything? The what? The blank sheet off the pad, what pad? Oh, all right, I'll come up. Yes, at once. Goodbye."

He settled his hat firmly on his head, avoided the porter's eye and went out to pick up a taxi. When it drew up at the house in the Rue Olive the door opened before he had had time to knock and Giselle put her head out. Curtains also moved slightly at the windows of adjacent houses; on the first floor of the house next door a face appeared, so pressed against the pane that its nose showed white in the light from a street-lamp opposite.

Hambledon thanked his stars that he did not live in Brussels and went quickly indoors.

It appeared that after the police had gone away with their prisoners Hambledon and Maurice, Brigitte woke up Giselle and they made themselves some coffee before going up to bed. When they did, Brigitte took the stewpan with her just in case. "We were not nervous, m'sieu', but so many things had happened and it is as well to be prepared." They went to bed, both in the same room for company since the house was otherwise empty, and Brigitte was just dropping off to sleep when she heard a noise downstairs.

"I begged her not to go, m'sieu'," said Giselle. "I knelt to her, but you cannot turn Brigitte. She opens the door ever so quietly and creeps down the stairs. Me, I stay on the landing and look over the banisters."

"Had you got your weapon with you?" asked Tommy.

Brigitte said scornfully that of course she had. She opened the kitchen door and there was a man with a torch in one hand and a piece of paper in the other. He was holding it sideways to the light and apparently trying to read something written on it. He looked up, saw her and straightway rushed to the window and scrambled out. He was a man between forty and fifty, with dark eyes and black hair turning grey. "I could not catch him to hit him, m'sieu'. I threw the pot at him and it broke in pieces in the yard outside. He ran away. This is all there is left," said Brigitte sadly, and showed the long handle with a jagged star of cast iron on the end. "We have lost our pot."

"And all the neighbours woke up," said Giselle, "and looked out of the windows and asked what we were doing making such noises in a respectable neighbourhood at that time of night. They were rude."

"Here is the pad," said Brigitte.

The pad was that on which Hambledon had written his note for the police sergeant, and there was a ragged strip across the top which had not been there before. It was thin paper of poor quality and Hambledon had written on it with a hard pencil. He turned the pad sideways to the light, it was almost possible to read the message on the next sheet; on the one which had been removed it must have been quite plain.

"He took the piece of paper with him, did he?"

"Yes, m'sieu'. He could read what you wrote before, no doubt. I should have put it away," said Brigitte.

"But how did he know," asked Giselle, "that m'sieu' had written anything on the paper?"

"I don't know," said Tommy, "unless he was watching from outside all the time." Giselle gave a little squeal of horror and Hambledon said there was a hole in the curtain.

"Tomorrow I mend it," said Brigitte.

"And a new catch for the window," said Giselle. "It has been broken for weeks, that catch."

"Tonight we will wedge it," said Hambledon. He cut a couple of wedges out of firewood and hammered them home with the head of the poker.

"The writing," said Brigitte. "Was it important?"

"Nothing desperate," said Hambledon. "I'd rather he hadn't read it but it doesn't really matter. You did not know him, Brigitte? Never mind, I don't suppose you've missed much. I'm sorry about your pot but you've still got a lovely weapon, haven't you? It reminds me of the sort of thing people used to hit each other with in the Middle Ages. There is something faintly mediaeval about you, Brigitte. By the way, I'm going to Paris tomorrow for a few days so if you get into any more trouble, ring up the police. You'll find them quite helpful, I've been talking to them. Lock the front door after me and go straight to bed, it's nearly three o'clock and soon it won't be worth while going to bed at all. Where's my hat—oh, here. Goodbye, Brigitte; goodbye, Giselle. What a night, but at least it isn't raining. Goodnight."

"But, m'sieu'——"

"What?"

"You will be returning to Brussels?"

"Oh, I expect so. I should think there's no doubt about it. We didn't get to the pictures tonight after all, did we? When I come back, we will. Thank you very much for all you've done for me. Goodnight."

Hambledon removed himself hastily from the house since Giselle showed signs of a tendency to become tearful, and walked quickly back to the hotel. In the hall there was, naturally, the night porter.

"If the part of this hotel in which my bedroom is situated should catch fire," said Hambledon, "you may call me, but not otherwise. Understood?"

"Perfectly, m'sieu'. Fire in any other part——"

"Is of no interest. Goodnight."

"And as regards telephone calls, m'sieu'——"

"The same applies."

"Perfectly, m'sieu'."

VII

THE BAKER'S BOY

WHEN the waiter in the Terminus Cafe fired at the young man who had tried to steal Hambledon's parcel the bullet merely grazed his skull, cutting a groove in the scalp which bled profusely, but otherwise producing much the same effect as if someone had hit him on the head with something hard. He was stunned for a few minutes; he began to revive when he was carried down the stairs; when he was conveyed into an empty store-room and dropped on the floor he was conscious enough to hear the key turn in the lock and the departing foot-steps of his bearers. The store-room was not quite dark since there was a fan-light over the door and a light in the passage outside. He sat up unsteadily and dabbed delicately with his handkerchief at the cut on his head which was atrociously painful besides being quite horribly messy. Giselle had described him as an apache; indeed he had looked the part in a rather flashy suit, a dark scarf round his neck instead of a collar, a wide-peaked cloth cap pulled down over one eye and a consciously sinister expression. Here, sitting miserably on a damp brick floor, it was apparent that he was much younger and much less experienced than he had pretended to be. The corners of his mouth drooped and his chest heaved with breaths which were very near being sobs, he sniffed unhappily and smeared his face with blood from the handkerchief when he tried to blow his nose. Altogether he looked like an extremely naughty small boy who has done something quite outrageous and met with a reprisal which has shaken him to the core.

He struggled to his feet with the help of the wall and switched the light on with some idea of trying to tidy himself up, but the room was quite unfurnished except for some empty packing-cases. Not even a sack he could wipe his hands on, let alone a water-tap. The key turned quietly in the lock, the boy staggered as he turned to see who had come in. It was a middle-aged man dressed like a better-class workman in his Sunday suit; the boy knew him at once and had known him for years.

"Burenne! What—why are you here?"

"Can you walk? You've got to, we're getting out of here. Put your scarf over your head, people will think you've got toothache. That's right," said Burenne, arranging the scarf over the boy's head and tucking the ends into his coat. "Now. If no one's about——"

Burenne opened the door a crack and listened, opened it wider and looked out. The passage was empty and the outer door only five steps away.

"Now then!"

Burenne pulled the boy out of the room by the arm, shut the door and turned the key, and then hustled him through the outer door and up the service stairs to the street.

"Hold up, I've got you. Got a car just along here. Come on, march!"

By sheer luck they met no policeman in the fifty yards

along the street to the place where Burenne's shabby little saloon was parked, and if any of the passers-by peered at them a little too closely Burenne's running commentary about how much better one feels when the tooth is, at last, out, disarmed curiosity. The boy crawled into the back seat with a sob of relief and was covered up with a horse-blanket.

"What you want," said Burenne, "is a cup of coffee."

He drove to a cafe in a quiet street and brought a cup of coffee out to his patient who sipped it and revived visibly.

"Have another?"

"Yes, please."

Burenne brought another coffee for the boy and a glass of wine for himself, and sat in the car for what he called "a little conversation between us. In the first place," he began, "how long have you been in Brussels?"

"Five days."

"I heard that you had left home and no one knew where you had gone. Then I look into that cafe from the street and see you holding up the patron with a gun. Why, if one may ask?"

"I had to have that parcel."

"Just Heaven, so I saw for myself. Why did you want the parcel?"

No answer.

"Jules Parisot, what was in the parcel?"

"I—I—oh, my head aches!"

"Serve you right," said Burenne, but not unkindly. "What was in the parcel?"

"Belgian franc notes," said Parisot in a whisper.

"Good ones?"

"No."

"So you did know what you were doing, you drivelling young idiot. You know what the penalty for that is, don't you? Transportation. Penal Colony."

The boy shrank back into his corner.

"And if I hadn't turned up at just the right moment like a super-sports chromium-plated Guardian Angel, that's what *you'd* have got. Well?"

"I am grateful," gulped Parisot.

"So you ought to be. Now then. Who brought you into this? Answer me!"

"Maurice."

Burenne muttered something and stared absently out of the car window for some minutes.

"So it was Maurice, was it? He sent you in there to pull his chestnuts out of the fire for him, eh? And stood outside to watch his puppy dog perform. Eh?"

"He—I don't think he was there."

"Oh yes, he was. When you fell down he dived in, grabbed the parcel and ran for it. *He* got away."

Burenne paused for a moment to let this sink in.

"Now tell me, where did you get to know Maurice? Last I heard of you you were at Boissy-le-Bel between the river and the forest, making the bread for Papa Canot while Francine, at the table under the window, rolled out the pastries. Eh?"

Burenne received no answer and perhaps did not expect one. He rearranged his feet on the seat beside him, lit a cigarette and went on talking.

"Not a bad spot, Boissy-le-Bel, if you like the country. I'm not so set on it, myself, not in winter anyway. Of course, you can always run up to Paris and take your girl to the pictures or do a bit of window-shopping in the Rue de Rivoli, it's the only sort of shopping you ever would do in that street. Still, it passes the time, don't it? 'If I was rich, Francine, I'd buy you that ermine cloak.' 'No thanks for ermine, Jules, for me it is mink or nothing.' Eh? Then you go and hold hands in the Tuileries Gardens till it's time to catch the bus back to Boissy-le-Bel beside the forest, and when you get out of the bus it's dark but you know exactly where you are because you can smell the roses in the postmaster's garden. That is, if you like smelling roses."

Burenne paused again. It was dark in the car and he could not see his passenger's face, but there was a rhythmic snuffling sound in the back seat, suppressed but audible, which appeared to satisfy him for he nodded slightly.

"Instead of which," he went on in a sterner tone, "here I find you holding up respectable restaurant patrons with a gun which is so big and clumsy that when you have to take a parcel you must drop the gun to do so. Then somebody naturally picks up the gun and shoots you with it. Name of a small blue dog, what else did you expect? Now you have a crack on the head which is less than you deserve, and the police are after you, naturally, and your friend Maurice has run off and left you and very sensible of him too, and have you got any money? Seven francs fifty? Kind Heaven, he is two hundred miles from home and all the money he has got is seven francs fifty. But what do you propose to do?"

"I cannot go home," sobbed Parisot. "I am ashamed."

"You want to go home, do you? You really prefer it to all this? You are quite sure about that? Very well, stop blubbering and answer my questions."

Burenne was told the incoherent outlines of a story about how Jules and Francine had gone to Paris for the day and had a quarrel so violent that Francine went home and left him in the middle of the afternoon. He walked miserably about by himself and eventually found himself in a pot-house in the Montmartre quarter with a gang of fellows who laughed at him for being such a sissy as to work hours every day—work!—for a splay-fingered baker for a handful of francs a week when one could get money, real money, by just being a bit smarter than the other guys. What time did he get up in the morning? At half-past three? Why, that was when a real guy was thinking of going to bed. This was the life, and so on. Then they played cards and he won, which proved that he was capable of something better than dough-thumping. He had various things to drink which affected him in a manner which surprised him; he woke up next morning in somebody's flat with a sense of being no end of a lad in spite of a hang-over. He returned to Boissy-le-Bel at about midday, had a real tongue-lashing from Papa Canot and Francine would not look at him. So he rattled the money in his pocket, more than he had ever had at one time before, defied Papa Canot, packed his bag and went back to his new friends in Paris. Papa Canot waited a few days and then went to the police about him; not that he wished to make any charge against young Parisot but because the boy was an orphan and might be led away into evil courses. His new friends heard about this and hid him away from the police, which was rather fun while it lasted, but he ran out of money and things became less pleasant. Maurice, whom he had met by now, said that if he wanted to do something to earn his keep there was a little job in Brussels where Maurice could do with an assistant. So Jules came to Brussels.

"I see. Where are you living?"

"Different places. Just rooms for the night."

"Where does Maurice hang out?"

"Bungalow place almost in the country, out beyond Laeken. I've been there several times."

"Good. We will go there. You will pilot me."

"But, if Maurice is there——"

"I do not care whether Maurice is there or not. If he is I have a word or two to say to him. If he's not we will manage quite well without him."

Since they were then in one of the small streets behind the Botanical Gardens the most direct route was along the Rue Olive. Young Parisot peered out when they drew near the house where Brigitte lived; he was about to say that that was one of the houses he had visited on Maurice's orders when he noticed a car standing outside, it was an old Citroën.

"That car there," he said. "It's Maurice's."

"The devil it is! What house is that, do you know?"

Jules explained while Burenne slowed the car and turned it into the next side street. "But why are you stopping?"

"I am curious. Is there a back entrance to that house?"

"Maurice said so, I haven't been there. Down by a synagogue into a yard at the back."

Burenne got out of the car. "You stay where you are till I come back, don't get out whatever you do. You go to sleep." He walked quickly round the block of houses and arrived in the yard in time to see, through the tear in the blind, Maurice sitting on the floor tenderly exploring

96

a bump on his head while a short stout girl with a determined expression was pointing a small automatic at his midriff. Another girl, tall and thin, was standing by the stove enjoying the scene and Burenne, in spirit, was with her. A delicious sight, and he might so easily have missed it.

The room door swung open and a man walked in, smiling; a man of Burenne's own age, broad shouldered and spare in figure. Burenne took one look at his clothes and said to himself that the gentleman was English. He did not recognize Hambledon at all since he had only seen him hurriedly as a dark silhouette at the entrance to the dark archway where Yanni the Nephew lay dead. Hambledon took the automatic from the short girl and perched on the edge of the kitchen table to keep guard over Maurice. They were talking, though what they said was infuriatingly inaudible outside the window, and Burenne was afire with curiosity. Hambledon took a cigarette-case from his pocket with his left hand, the tall girl took out a cigarette and put it between his lips while the short girl provided a lighted match. They were enjoying themselves, that was plain, all except Maurice who looked increasingly miserable. Time passed and nothing particular happened.

"They are waiting for something," Burenne guessed correctly. "Or somebody."

Before Hambledon's cigarette was finished there came a loud knocking at the front door, Burenne in the yard behind heard it easily. The tall girl clapped her hands derisively at Maurice and ran out of the room; she returned a moment later with a sergeant of police and a constable.

"But this is magnificent," said Burenne, and watched

enthralled as the drama unrolled. The sergeant sat at the table and made notes while Maurice lolled against the wall with the constable brooding over him. First one girl spoke, then the other, and finally the Englishman. What was this? The sergeant did not appear to like the Englishman. Burenne was most indignant; anyone who could beat up Maurice and then hand him over to the police was a person to be esteemed. More, encouraged. Hambledon never knew how near he was to being rescued then and there but that Burenne had reasons for not wishing to encounter the police. A dead man in one of the arches of a railway bridge, for one, since he had been fool enough to drop his gun there. It would have his prints on it; Burenne had a quite superstitious belief in the fatality of finger-prints.

Hambledon turned suddenly to Brigitte who tore open a dresser drawer and gave him a writing-pad and a pencil. He began to write, looked doubtfully at the pencil, and could be seen to press more heavily. It was a short message, he tore it off and gave it to the sergeant who read it carefully and stowed it away in his wallet. The incredible scene ended with the sergeant handcuffing—actually handcuffing—the heroic Englishman to that putrescent muck-worm, Maurice. Burenne breathed so hard with indignation that he misted the glass through which he was peering. When he had wiped it clear again the police and their prisoners had gone, a moment later he heard the car start up and drive away. Two cars; they had taken also Maurice's Citroen.

The short girl looked towards a corner of the room which was outside Burenne's range of vision, she put her arms akimbo and spoke without, apparently, result; she dived out of sight and returned dragging by the wrist the tall girl who was rubbing her eyes with her free hand. They aimed playful slaps at each other, the short girl gave the long one a push towards the door and she went out. The short one then picked up a large and heavy stewpan with a long handle, gave a final glance round the room and went out also, switching off the light as she went. The play, it seemed, was over.

Burenne stood outside in the dark yard and thought about what he had seen. He had told Parisot the bare truth when he had said that he was habitually curious, a trait he shared with Hambledon. It had got him into quite enough trouble in the past but he was not cured and never would be. The Englishman, who was he, and what was the message he wrote? On thin paper, written with a hard pencil, it should be legible on the next sheet also if one held it sideways to the light. It might be very useful to know what the message was. He switched on a small electric torch he always carried and examined the window. It was of the ordinary sash type and the catch was broken; the sill was not more than four feet from the ground.

It took him some time to push up the sash without noise, it was ill-fitting and inclined to stick. At last he swung himself up into the room and tiptoed across to the table, but on his way he stepped on a loose board which creaked alarmingly when it took his weight and louder still when he leapt off it. Burenne was not a burglar by trade, he listened intently but could hear nothing but his pulses thumping. It was of no consequence, there were only two girls in the house and what are girls? Nothing. One can deal with girls.

He tore the top sheet off the pad and examined it by the light of his torch, the words were perfectly plain. "I am Thomas Elphinstone Hambledon of British Intelligence visiting Belgium on official business. Your Chief——"

The door opened without warning since Brigitte had come downstairs with bare feet, the light was switched on and Burenne looked up to see one of the Furies in person in the posture of attack. Her hair stood up, her eyes blazed, she showed her teeth and in her hand she brandished that appalling stewpan. She uttered a sound which was not a word but a snarl and took a step forward. Burenne's nerve broke, he turned and fled. He fell out of the window, picked himself up and ran as something heavy flew past his ear and smashed, with a frightful clatter, in the yard. He tore along the passage by the synagogue and was out in the street before windows went up round the yard and the neighbours began their commentary, but he still held his piece of paper.

He dropped into a walk and returned to his car. Jules Parisot, in the back seat, was not asleep but shivering with anxiety.

"I thought you were never coming——"

Burenne broke into a laugh. "I've been watching the funniest thing I've seen since I was a little boy and went to the circus. Clowns, bah, you can have clowns. First of all, Maurice has been arrested and taken off to clink so we need not to worry about him." He started the car, backed out into the Rue Olive and continued to drive towards Laeken, telling his story as he went.

Maurice inhabited a bungalow built on the edge of the city, where side streets became lanes and there were fields behind the gardens. The Parisot boy, much more confident now that he knew he would not meet Maurice, pointed out the house; Burenne drove a little past it and pulled off the road in the shadow of a clump of trees.

"Now to get in," he said.

"To get in so far is simple," said Jules. "There is a room at the back with a door to the garden and I have the key of that. He gave it me yesterday to come in this evening and wait for him. I have done that before, I forgot to give the key back. We were in there together when the telephone message came about getting that parcel from the two girls in the Avenue des Boulevards. We rushed out and then there was trouble with the car, she would not start——"

"What do you mean, 'so far'? If we are in the house we are in the house, are we not?"

"But the inner door of that room is locked always," explained Parisot. "I have never been past that door."

"We will deal with that door when we come to it," said Burenne, getting out of the car. "Come on, you. He has no one else in his house, I suppose?"

"I heard sweeping noises once and Maurice said it was the woman cleaning."

"The woman cleaning! Will she be there in the middle of the night? Use the intelligence the good God gave you, or has it all leaked out of the cut on your head?"

The boy thought it wiser not to answer. He led the way round to a door at the back, which he opened. It led into a small room furnished with a table, three or four chairs, an electric fire and a telephone.

"No safe," said Burenne, looking about him. "Nothing

here. Now let's look at this door." He drew a pair of gloves from his pocket and put them on.

It was an ordinary sitting-room door opening away from them, it had been fitted with a Yale lock but the door itself was of flimsy construction. Burenne had brought a tyre-lever from the car, he forced it between the door and the jamb and pulled it towards him. There was a splintering crash and, as the door swung open, a sort of babbling sound of terror which might at any moment become a scream.

"More women!" said Burenne, and rushed across a passage into a lighted room beyond. It was a bedroom and in it was a girl with masses of light fluffy hair and a pink silly face. She was sitting in front of her dressing-table on which, in addition to the usual array of toilet accessories, there was a French novel propped up and an open box of chocolates. She was wearing a flowered dressing-gown and was engaged in enamelling her finger-nails a vivid scarlet. At the sight of Burenne she opened her mouth wide for a real scream but he was too quick for her. He covered her mouth with one large hand, snatched a stocking from the back of a chair and expertly gagged her with it. Another stocking tied her hands together behind her back and the pink cord of the curtain-looper secured her feet. Parisot stood watching in the doorway, his expression a mixture of horror and admiration.

"You are quick," he said.

Burenne brushed past him and hurried round the house opening doors; the third one showed him what he wanted, the larder. He picked the girl up, carried her inside and dumped her down on the floor. The place was not much larger than a cupboard and had perforated zinc over the window. She emitted what can only be described as whining noises; Burenne backed out, shut the door and locked it.

"Now. Where would Maurice keep his money? Locked up somewhere away from that girl, I'll bet."

There was a handbag in the bedroom with a few hundred francs in it; Burenne, anxious to point a moral, such as it was, left them there.

"We'll only take those if we can't find anything else. It is Maurice who owes you compensation, not that blonde. This is not a robbery, it is a repayment. Remember that."

They crossed the passage into the sitting-room.

"I still don't see a safe," said Burenne. "Of course he could keep money in the stuffing of that sofa or under a loose floor-board. What is in that cabinet?"

Parisot tried the door of a tall imitation lacquer cabinet which stood between the windows but it was locked and he looked round for a key. Burenne pushed him aside.

"Go and get that tyre-lever, I dropped it in the passage."

The cabinet resisted the tyre-lever even less than the first door had done, it opened and there was a safe inside. Burenne looked at it doubtfully.

"If only I was a burglar," he began, but Parisot interrupted him.

"Listen! Someone coming!"

There was a flagged path from the road to the front door and steps were plainly to be heard coming up it, short steps, with the tapping of high-heeled shoes.

"Another woman," said Burenne resignedly. "This Maurice—that back door's still open."

He ran quietly through the house to shut and lock it and switch off the light, as he did so the front-door bell rang. He came back to find Parisot staring at the door, Burenne pushed him into the sitting-room out of sight.

"She might look through the letter-box," he explained in a whisper.

"She will see there's a light in here, won't she?"

"Can't help that. Let her think it's been left on by accident."

The bell rang again, a longer peal and more insistent. There was another pause and the woman outside rang a third time.

VIII

SLUSH

AFTER what seemed an interminable time but was possibly two minutes there came the welcome sound of footsteps retreating along the path; they stopped, the gate clicked, and silence followed.

"Now," said Burenne, "this safe. For the first time in my life," he added primly and quite untruthfully, "I wish I was a burglar. Do you know if he carried keys about in his pockets?"

Parisot shook his head and then winced. "I don't think so, except his latch-key, of course." He moved forward and saw himself in a mirror, the sight horrified him as well it might. "No wonder that girl wanted to scream," he said. "Have we time to permit me to wash?"

"But, certainly. We have what is left of the night before us and it may be that a wash will improve your wits. It assuredly will your face." Parisot walked into the kitchen and turned on the tap over the sink; Burenne wandered after him, still talking. "Maurice would not leave the key of his safe where that girl could get at it; it is even unlikely that she knows where it is, which is as well for her since otherwise she would have to tell us. Where, then, would he put it? Hidden, or locked up somewhere?"

"I remember now," said Parisot, removing a dripping

head from under the tap. "He had two keys on a ring, his latch-key and a little one." He indicated a key about an inch long. "He said it was the key of his money-box, his mother always brought him up to keep a money-box and like a good boy he did."

"I said cold water would improve your wits. Now we know what we are looking for. A money-box—perhaps. At least it may have money in it. Reparations, just like what we're taking off the Germans." Burenne looked quickly round the kitchen and said it was not likely to be there. "I'll go and look in the other bedroom. You come in when you're ready."

Young Parisot was drying himself on the roller towel and grunted in reply, the cut on his head was bleeding again and giving him trouble. He followed Burenne into the other bedroom, which was obviously Maurice's, and began looking in the dressing-table drawers. "Seen any sticking-plaster?" he asked. "I have it. Found anything?"

"Not yet," said Burenne with his head in the wardrobe.

"What about looking on the top?"

Burenne put his hand over the ornamental heading along the top and immediately encountered a tin box and a lot of dust.

"You have the beginnings of intelligence," he said in a surprised voice. "Also Maurice knows his girl. She does not dust the tops of furniture, that type." It was a tin cash-box of a cheap kind, and locked; Burenne shook it and was rewarded by a rattle. "That does not sound like coins," he said thoughtfully, and went for the tyre-lever.

But tyre-levers are not well adapted for opening tin cash-boxes and if it had been made of steel it might have defied them altogether. Before they got it open they had bent up Maurice's tin-opener, broken two knives off short at the handle and buckled the corners of the coke-shovel. Eventually Parisot hammered one end in with the head of the poker and the tyre-lever did the rest.

Inside, there were five thousand eight hundred francs, mainly in French currency, and a long slim key with a castellated head.

"Ah," said Burenne in a satisfied tone, and put the money in his pocket. "That will take us home and, of what there is left, you shall have some. You will need some for the ring, will you not? Francine will deserve a good one if she consents to take you back after all this."

"She will deserve also Eldorado," said the boy gloomily.

"Cheer up. Have you patched up your head? Let me look. Another piece across this way and all will be well, let me do it."

"Do you think that a clean collar and a handkerchief could be included in the reparations?"

"On this occasion," said Burenne solemnly, "I think so. It is a little undignified, that, to take a collar and a handkerchief; it is petty pilfering, the police would say. But you owe your injuries to him. Yes, take them. Yes, now you look at least clean and tidy again though the good God never meant you to be handsome, behold your nose. Now let us go and look at the safe. These notes are genuine, anyway."

Those in the safe definitely were not. There were hundreds of them of different values and of various currencies, all counted out and neatly banded together in packets. Burenne pulled out each packet separately, tore off the rubber bands which held it and ran hastily through it. A quick shake of the head and he threw the notes down on the floor where they floated apart and littered the carpet. "All slush," he said, "all slush," and took out another. In a quarter of an hour the room looked as though it had snowed currency notes and the men, as they moved about, shuffled through them as children kick through fallen leaves in autumn forests.

"Do you know," said Parisot suddenly, "it is nearly five o'clock and soon there will be people about?"

"You are right," said Burenne, "we will go. There is nothing here to interest honest men," and he did not even blush when he said it.

"What about the girl?"

"She'll be all right. Presently the police will come to search the house and they will find her. Don't leave any of your things behind, where's your collar? On the floor here, and as heaven looks down on us, there's 'Parisot' written inside. If that doesn't teach you to be honest, nothing will. I take my tyre-lever. Is there anything else? Switch the lights off and let us go. To Boissy-le-Bel, forward!"

Five hours later Hambledon was sitting in the police station while the Brussels police, with Letord's assistance, interrogated Maurice. They did not get very far and Tommy said to himself that that Maurice had been interrogated before, he knew the ropes, that type. He had nothing to do with any forged currency, of course not. He was confronted with Papa from the Rue Olive, they looked blankly at each other and said it was the first time they had met. In any case, Papa said he had no connection with the forged currency racket. At this point Hambledon gave evidence about following Yanni from the Taverne Gruber, finding him murdered and taking the mat with

Papa's address on it. Hambledon went on to describe how, with the able assistance of the eminent French detective M. Antoine Letord of the Sûreté, he had gone to the house in the Rue Olive, passed through a series of adventures and finally obtained the parcel of forged currency notes which the said M. Letord had handed to the police.

"The resourceful English M. 'Armbeeldon had an evening of the utmost excitement yesterday," said the Brussels Chief of Police with a polite bow.

"Oh, not 'utmost'," said Tommy modestly. "There were moments, but m'sieu' Letord dealt with them."

Papa said that the Englishman had indeed come to his house the previous evening and talked a great deal which was quite incomprehensible about a parcel until it dawned upon Papa that the explanation was simple. The Englishman had come to the wrong house.

"Did I, in fact, give you any parcel?"

"No," said Tommy. "You did not."

"You asked, did you not, for somebody named Raoul?"

"I did."

"Gentleman, not only have I no one of that name in my house but I do not even know anyone with that name."

"You don't have to," said Letord bluntly. "Raoul is not in this instance the name of any particular person. It is a password."

"Password? Password? What has a poor old man like me to do with passwords? I am a tailor, for my living I make buttonholes. All my life I have made buttonholes and never once have I found a password necessary. These buttonholes, they do not——"

The Chief of Police interrupted him.

"Cease to pretend an idiocy. You gave the parcel to the two girls, we have heard their testimony. You told them to——"

Papa intervened with character-sketches of Giselle and Brigitte which earned him the rebuke of the Court, and rightly, but not before the girls had risen in their places and had to be forcibly restrained by the police. Papa apologized.

"I regret," he said, "the use of words which I should not have permitted myself to utter in honourable company. The ingratitude! I have looked after these girls like daughters and I will say at once that they took some looking after. They have become entangled in this currency villainy, some evilly-disposed young man of their acquaintance gave them the parcel to hand to who knows whom? When they are caught with it, they put the blame on me. Me, who have been like a father——" Papa wept.

The Chief of Police hammered upon his desk and demanded silence. "We are not enquiring into the manners or morals of the two female witnesses," he said severely, "at least, not at the moment," at which Maurice laughed. "Silence, prisoner. Now, old man, you say that the Englishman came to your house by mistake. Is that a good reason, even if true, for threatening him with a pistol?"

"Pistol?" said Papa, staring. "I have never owned a pistol."

"I did not say you owned it. You threatened the Englishman with one. So also did your vile accomplice, the fish-porter Schaer."

"Oh no," babbled Papa. "No, no, no. I am not habituated to fire-arms. What is this dreadful accusation? Did the police, then, find a pistol in my possession?"

"Artful old devil," said Hambledon in Letord's ear, for it was quite true that they had not. One of the Jews had disarmed Papa and pocketed the weapon. He was expecting to go to Palestine and it might prove useful.

"You are here to answer questions, not to ask them. You menaced the Englishman, both of you. Why?"

"No, sir. Schaer happened to come in while the Englishman and I were talking. When it was made clear that he had come to the wrong house we said that we would set him on his way and perhaps have a little glass together. So we three went out together and then, all for no reason, the Jews attacked us."

"That is your story, is it? The Englishman says otherwise and he is a witness of credit which is more than can be said for you. He holds very high office in his own country."

"Am I, then," said the old man passionately, "to be expected to explain the sayings of Englishmen whom all the world knows to be mad, however highly placed? Let me, rather, be confined in jail where the rules are simple and one is not confounded with conundrums."

"By the way," said Hambledon to Letord, "where is the amiable Schaer?"

"In hospital. His jaw was broken."

"You are a liar," thundered the Chief of Police. "I have another witness of whom you know nothing. Antoine Letord!"

Letord gave a short and business-like account of what he had seen through the window of Papa's kitchen; Schaer coming in with a revolver, Papa producing his pistol, and so on. Papa wilted visibly and turned green.

"I do not feel well," he said. "I have a spasm at the heart. Are you Christians? I wish to see a doctor."

"Remove him," said the Chief of Police. "We can have him back later, I have more to say to him. Much more." He turned to Maurice. "Now then, you. You have been several times to that house in the Rue Olive, you were seen to leave parcels there."

"No," said Maurice.

"You were, I say. It is useless to deny it, I have witnesses."

"What, those girls?" said Maurice, and laughed.

"What was in the parcels?"

"The ones I didn't leave? I don't know."

"You stole a parcel from the Terminus Cafe last night——"

"Oh, that. I plead guilty to that. It contained two pairs of flannel trousers in need of cleaning, and a tweed jacket, rather a nice one. For the sport, you know."

"You rushed into a respectable cafe and stole a parcel containing gentlemen's clothing. You admit that?"

"Certainly," said Maurice.

"Why did you do that?"

"I was passing by and saw a young man come from the back of the cafe and demand this parcel at the point of a revolver. The parcel fell down and, for a moment, nobody regarded it. I ask myself what there can be inside it that men go to such desperate lengths to obtain it. I took it in order to find out, that is all, m'sieu'. As to why any man not noticeably mentally deficient should go to those lengths to obtain a jacket and two pairs of trousers, that is quite beyond me, I admit it. I admit my guilt also."

"Where are these clothes now?"

"I gave them to the attendant in charge of the cloak-rooms under the Place Rogier."

The Chief of Police gave orders for enquiries to be made and continued his questions.

"Where do you live?"

"In Paris."

Letord, asking for fuller details, received answers which he did not believe, and the examination continued.

"Where do you live in Brussels?"

"I do not live in Brussels. I am here on a short vacation, that is all. I take a room for the night at the nearest hotel wherever I happen to be."

"How long have you been in Brussels?"

"Three days."

"They aren't getting much further with this fellow, are they?" said Hambledon in Letord's ear.

"What would you expect? He is, after all, Parisian."

"We turn now to the affair last night. You are accused of menacing with a fire-arm the two young women who live in the house in the Rue Olive which——"

Maurice threw his head back and burst into peals of laughter.

"Silence, prisoner!"

"There is something the matter with this house in the Rue Olive," he explained, still bubbling with amusement. "No matter who goes there or for what purpose——" he glanced at the girls—"before there has been time to say 'good evening, how is your health' out come the guns. First, apparently, this Englishman, and now me. It is true that he menaced me with an automatic, but, for the rest, it is not to be believed. It is the Wild West at the cinema, it is not real. It is, in short, too much. Your

profound commonsense, m'sieu', as a man of the
world——"

"Do you deny that your behaviour was such as to cause
one of these young women to defend herself with a kitchen
utensil?"

Maurice burst out laughing again and the police could
not stop him; one or two of them smiled covertly behind
their hands. He rubbed his head ruefully, saying, "I admit
the frying-pan episode," and laughed again. Giselle stood
up and said that if this scoundrel was to be allowed to
make suggestions against the moral character of herself
and her friend they would go out, with or without permission. The police must stop him. But the Chief of
Police was not listening because one of his Inspectors was
whispering in his ear. He stood up and said that the enquiry would be adjourned for half an hour; the prisoner
could be removed but the witnesses must wait. He then
beckoned to Letord and Hambledon who followed him
into his private room.

"Something has happened?"

"It is beyond belief, but Colette Masurel—you remember the letter signed Colette which was found in Maurice's
possession—she is here. She is anxious about her Maurice,
she has been to his house and found suspicious cir-
cucmstances——"

"His house, eh?" said Letord.

"Precisely. I thought that both you gentlemen might
wish to hear what she has to say."

Hambledon said that his friend's courtesy and co-opera-
tion exceeded everything but his inability adequately to
express his appreciation of it, Letord concurred, the Chief
of Police bowed, and Colette Masurel was ushered in. She

was a dark-haired woman in her early thirties, neatly if inexpensively dressed. She explained that she was the fiancee of Alexandre Maurice, at present in Brussels on business; at least, she understood that he was still in Brussels but she had received no reply to her last three letters. Becoming uneasy as to his well-being she had come in person to make enquiries and had called at his house.

"The address of this house, Mademoiselle?"

She gave the address of the bungalow. She had gone there, late as it was—between two and three o'clock in the morning—there had been a small accident on the line near the frontier and all the trains were two hours late——

"This was this morning? Eight or nine hours ago?"

She agreed. She had gone to the front door and rung the bell, there was a light in one of the rooms and she thought she heard someone moving about. Also a curious noise which was rather like a dog whining but not quite. However, no one answered the door although she rang twice more so she returned to the centre of the city and went to an hotel for what was left of the night. Fatigued with her journey, she overslept herself and it was after ten o'clock when she returned to the bungalow. The curtains were still closely drawn although there was no longer a light in the room which had been lit the night before, there was still no reply when she rang the bell and all the doors and windows were fastened. "I admit frankly, m'sieu', I went all round the house trying to get in and could not." What finally raised her anxiety to incandescence was that the whining sound began again accompanied by a bumping noise. "There is someone or something shut up there, m'sieu', and I do not think it is a dog. If it were my Alexandre! So I come to you."

The Chief of Police said with unaffected enthusiasm that she had done exactly the right thing, exactly, and that the correctness of her actions was a proof, if any were needed, of her undoubted intelligence. He added that if she would have the goodness to wait he would enquire into the matter in person, at once, and he swept Hambledon and Letord out of the room and into a police car before she had any opportunity to say that she wanted to come too.

They found the bungalow as she described it, locked up and curtained; they rang the front-door bell largely as a matter of form and waited for an answer.

"Listen," said Hambledon.

"The whining sound," said the Chief of Police. "She was right, that woman."

Letord cast round with his head on one side like a rotund but alert terrier and came to a stop at a small window covered with perforated zinc. It was firmly shut and it was quite impossible to see inside.

"It comes from here," he said.

"The larder?" suggested the Chief. "Courage!" he called. "We are coming!"

"Windows," said Hambledon, "are easier to open, as a rule, than doors."

"Especially," said Letord, "when one has the authority of the police to break a window-pane." He put his elbow through one of the sitting-room windows and undid the catch.

"It will be interesting," said the Chief of Police, climbing heavily over the sill, "to see who is in that larder. We have one advantage over the woman Masurel, we do at least know that it is not Maurice." He straightened himself, threw back the curtains, and immediately uttered a long and complicated oath.

"What is it?" said Hambledon and scrambled in after him, followed by Letord. The floor was littered with currency notes; on their right between the windows was an open cabinet containing a safe, also open, with the key still in the keyhole. The notes upon the floor had apparently come from this safe since there was still an odd packet or so left upon the shelves. Letord snatched up samples here and there and peered at them with his small magnifying-glass.

"Slush," he said, unconsciously echoing Burenne, "all slush."

"If the woman Masurel told the truth when she said this was the house of Alexandre Maurice," said the Chief of Police, "he will have some awkward questions to answer. She was right, I think, in what she said in her letter."

"He will in any case, won't he?" said Hambledon cheerfully. "Letord, it does look as though we have found something here."

"Beautifully made," said Letord, scrutinizing a French hundred-franc note. "These people, whoever they are, are artists. Here are some which will interest you, m'sieu'." They were allegedly English one-pound treasury notes and Hambledon examined them closely.

"Very artistic. You see they are all soiled and crumpled in the same way? The makers have even invented a machine for giving them that much-used appearance which is so helpful in covering up deficiencies."

The Chief of Police sidled round the room, making for the door. "The imprisoned one," he said, "can perhaps help us with a little information." He went out of the room and Hambledon went after him. There were several doors in the passage but they were all open except one which had a key in its lock. The Chief of Police unlocked it, threw it open, and a brightly-coloured bundle rolled out at his feet.

"A girl," said Tommy, "and gagged as well as bound. All right, all right, don't kick." He untied the gag and unwound the stocking from her face while the Chief of Police untied her hands and feet. "There now, that's better, isn't it?"

She threw herself flat, drummed with her heels on the floor and went into violent hysterics.

IX

UNSUCCESSFUL EXPERIMENT

THOMAS ELPHINSTONE HAMBLEDON said in a loud firm voice that he would fetch some water from the kitchen. He found the kitchen without difficulty but was unavoidably delayed in returning with the water until the yelps and squeals in the passage had ceased. He was occasionally attracted by women, but when they had (*a*) scarlet finger-nails and (*b*) hysterics he regarded them as practically sub-human. The noises ceased suddenly because Letord abandoned his false currency and came out in the passage. He found the girl rolling on the floor uttering the equivalent of Ha-ha and Boo-hoo alternately while the Chief of Police loomed over her like a cloud and ordered her to stop. Letord seized her by the wrist, dragged her into a sitting position and boxed her ears with energy and enthusiasm.

"Oh-oh! You hurt me!"

"Yes, and if you make that horrible noise again I'll slap you again. Harder. Get up."

He pulled her to her feet, walked her into her bedroom and sat her down on an upright chair. The Chief of Police continued the enquiry.

"Now then! Who did this to you?"

She didn't know. Two dreadful men. Bandits. Assassins.

"Well, they haven't assassinated you. Ah, here is some-one with a glass of water. Would you like a drink?"

She said that the delicacy of her system under the in-fluence of the horrible events of the past night really de-manded cognac.

"Presently, perhaps. Not yet. These men, what did they look like?"

They were about seven feet high with gleaming eye-balls and teeth, they were armed with knives and pistols, they burst into the house without warning, uttering hoarse cries, seized upon her in spite of her heroic defence, bound her brutally and thrust her into the larder.

"I believe that last bit, anyway. Can you describe these men at all?"

But it soon became clear that she did not know whether they were dark or fair, hairy or clean-shaven, or how they were dressed except that one wore a cloth cap and the other a felt hat and she was almost sure one was older than the other. Letord looked at Hambledon who made a little gesture with his glass of water indicating what he would like to do with it. The Belgian struggled on.

"If you saw them again, Mademoiselle, would you recognize them?"

"If I saw them even once more, m'sieu', I should die!"

"Well, let's try something else for a few moments until you are calmer. Your name?"

"Leonie Maurice. Madame Maurice."

"Oh. And your husband?"

"My husband is a dealer in wines and a man of the ut-most respectability."

"Without doubt, madame. And he lives here with you?"

"But, naturally! Are you suggesting——"

"Nothing, madame, nothing. It is only that he does not appear to be at home tonight."

"He is frequently away, on business, sometimes at very short notice, and returns with equal suddenness. I am expecting him at any moment."

"I see. Now, there is a safe in the next room. Is that the property of M. Alexandre Maurice?"

There was a moment's pause, she glanced down at the floor before she answered. "All the furniture in this house is my husband's, m'sieu', no doubt the safe also, with the rest."

"And its contents, madame?"

"As to the contents, I know nothing. It is no part of a wife's duty, m'sieu', to meddle with her husband's business." She rolled large blue eyes at the Chief of Police and her voice became suddenly childish and confidential. "Besides, I'm much too silly to understand business. If I do ask him anything he calls me his Little Snowdrop and says it's my business to be beautiful and leave real clever business to him. So I do, naturally. Wouldn't you?"

"It is your opinion, madame, that the contents of the safe are your husband's property?"

"Oh, I wouldn't know anything like that! I suppose he might put something in there for one of his friends sometimes, if the friend asked him to keep it safe? You must ask Alexandre."

"I agree, madame. I will ask him. Now, you have had a severe shock. My instructions are that you lie down upon your bed in here and rest until I return. I will leave a police officer in the house so you will be quite safe. For half an hour, madame, that is all. Rest, essential rest," he urged, backing out of the room preceded by Hambledon and Letord, and shut the door behind him. It then appeared that the key of the bedroom door had slipped out of the keyhole into Hambledon's hand as he passed it, and the door was locked on the outside.

"She will get out of the window," said Letord.

"Not with my police driver on duty outside. We will drive ourselves back, gentlemen."

At the police station Maurice was brought from his cell to the Chief's private office.

"You stated, Maurice, in reply to a question, that you had no fixed address in Brussels. Is that correct?"

"Perfectly correct."

"And that you have only been here for a few days?"

"Correct again."

"Indeed. Inspector! An escort for the prisoner in the car. We are going for a little ride, Maurice."

"Charmed, of course," drawled Maurice, and swaggered out in charge of a constable.

"Will he brazen it out, do you suppose?" asked the Belgian, but Letord only shrugged his shoulders. "And the girl, what did you think of her, M. Hambledon? I asked you that in the car but I do not think you heard me."

"I was probably engaged in prayer," said Tommy. "Your driving, m'sieu', has all the virtues, including that of reminding a man of his sins."

"I make you nervous, eh? I am sorry. It is not so dangerous as it looks, when people see me coming they get out of my way."

"But suppose," urged Tommy, "that one day you meet some imbecile who fails to recognize you?"

"Then I shall instantly arrest him," said the Belgian,

laughing, and led the way out to the car. Letord followed and Hambledon, with his hands lightly clasped together, brought up the rear. Maurice sat in the back seat with a constable on one side of him and Letord upon the other. Hambledon, sitting in front beside the Chief of Police, turned in his seat when the journey neared its end, ostensibly to speak to Letord but covertly to watch Maurice's face when it became evident to which house they were going. He might have saved himself the trouble; the prisoner showed no emotion of any kind, not even interest.

They went up the path and into the house together. In the passage the Chief of Police held Maurice with one hand, unlocked the bedroom door with the other and hustled him inside. There was a squeal of joy from within but it suddenly tailed off in mid-screech.

"I have brought you your husband, madame," said the Belgian.

"What? No, m'sieu', this is not my husband. He is a little like him, it is true, I myself was deceived in the first moment. But no, that is not my Alexandre."

"Very neat," said Hambledon in Letord's ear. "See what he did? Made a face at her at exactly the moment when the Chief looked away. I saw it myself. Very quick and cool."

"Rascal though he is," said Letord complacently, "he is yet Parisian."

"And the girl isn't so silly as she likes to look," added Tommy.

"These women," murmured Letord, "are they ever? It is the ones who try to look clever whom one may disregard. I, Letord, have had my experiences."

Inside the room there was an argument in progress. The

girl said the prisoner was not Alexandre Maurice; Maurice said that he was; but not, of course, the one who had the happiness to be married to the lady whose bedroom had been so uncivilly invaded. On behalf of men of honour of all nations, he apologized for the manners of the Belgian police. He himself would never have presumed——

"Why doesn't the Chief stop this?" said Hambledon. "Maurice's fingerprints are doubtless all over the flat."

"Wants them to talk," said Letord, with a shrug. At that point the Chief apparently gave it up as a bad job. He brought Maurice out of the room and sent him to sit in the small room leading to the garden with the constable escort to keep him company. The Chief then stalked out of the house and had a word with the police driver who had been left on guard. The man saluted and went down the path at a run.

"I have sent for the other woman," said the Chief. "Then we shall, perhaps, see something."

"An illuminating display of fireworks?" suggested Hambledon, and went to help Letord clear up the sitting-room floor of its spurious wealth. They packed it back into the safe which, said Letord, would be removed bodily as evidence. There was nothing else in the safe, "not even the accounts of his alleged business as a wine-merchant, m'sieu'."

"Not even a few samples," grunted Hambledon.

They had not long finished when the police car pulled up at the gate and the driver came up the path at the elbow of Colette Masurel. The Chief of Police welcomed her in a few stately phrases and bowed her to the most comfortable chair in the sitting-room.

"You have been in this house before, mademoiselle?"

"Never, no. I did but know it as an address."

He nodded and went out of the room to return a moment later with the golden-haired Leonie. She had improved the time of waiting by getting completely dressed in a street suit, making up her face, doing her hair and attaching to one side of it an alleged hat consisting of two pink roses, a pinch of black lace and a bright blue canary. The two women eyed each other with raised eyebrows, bowed in a detached manner and looked fixedly elsewhere. The Chief of Police arranged Leonie in a chair facing Colette's and once more went out of the room, shutting the door behind him. There was at least five minutes of unbroken silence during which Colette, her hands quietly at rest in her lap, gazed steadily out of the window, Leonie began to fidget, Letord looked from one to the other and Hambledon repressed a growing desire to laugh.

At last the door opened and the Chief of Police came in followed by Maurice with his constable escort at his elbow. Leonie sat tight but Colette leapt to her feet.

"My Alexandre! But what is this that they have done to thee?"

She pushed past the Chief, who made way for her, and throwing her arms round Maurice's neck, pressed her cheek to his, murmuring endearments. Leonie rose slowly and stiffly from her chair, visibly quivering, but did not speak; perhaps words were for the moment denied her. Besides, Maurice managed to throw her an imploring glance which should have softened a statue while furtively patting Colette on the shoulder which he hoped Leonie could not see. His face was quite white and beads of perspiration stood on his forehead, he whispered something to Colette and tried to withdraw from her.

"What?" she cried. "A prisoner? Oh, no. Of what have they accused my man?"

This removed Leonie instantly far beyond the reach of imploring glances and she drew herself up to every inch of her five feet four inches.

"Will someone," she said, looking imperiously round the room, "be so polite as to tell me who is this woman who has come to my house?"

"Your house!" said Colette, wheeling upon her. Then, with a little laugh, "Of course, how stupid I am! She is thy landlady, most dearest. She lets rooms, it proclaims itself. Your pardon, madame, I beg, I am agitated, I am not myself. *Cheri*, I hope she attended adequately to all thy requirements. Thy so delicate stomach, can she cook?"

Maurice unconsciously produced a faint moaning noise between his teeth but Leonie actually hissed like a kettle coming to the boil.

"Just once more, who is this woman?"

"I understand," said the Chief of Police in his blandest voice, "that this lady is the devoted fiancee of M. Alexandre Maurice. Driven by natural anxiety for his welfare, she has come from Paris——"

"Fiancee!" shrieked Leonie. "Impossible!"

Maurice engaged in audible prayer but Colette, tall and dignified, advanced upon Leonie.

"Impossible? And why?"

"Because he is my husband! How dare——"

Colette remarked to the room in general that it would be interesting to see the lady's alleged marriage certificate.

Leonie said that it was doubtful, in her opinion, whether Colette had ever seen such a thing even in her childhood's home. For some reason this stung Colette who abandoned dignity to cling to Maurice and beg to be assured that he had not, indeed and truly not, married this yellow-haired, painted, conscienceless——

"Detach thyself!" screamed Leonie. "My husband is not for such as thee!"

She entangled her fingers in Colette's smooth dark hair and tugged viciously, Colette swung round and drew her finger-nails down Leonie's cheek, leaving four red lines.

"Now they're off," said Letord dispassionately.

"Ladies! Ladies!" thundered the Chief of Police. "Do you now deny, madame, that this is your husband Alexandre Maurice?"

"How dare you!" snapped Colette, and boxed the big Belgian's ears. This was a mistake because it distracted her attention from Leonie who uttered a shriek of rage, sprang at Colette and proceeded to try to strangle her. Maurice's constable escort sprang forward automatically to the help of his chief, the two women rolled on the floor and the prisoner, with a wail of fear, opened the door and ran like a terrified cat. Before anyone realized what was happening or could get to the door to stop him he had run through to the back of the house and out, across the garden, leaping the fence at the end and away through market gardens and orchards to freedom.

The constable escort and the police driver pursued him but in vain. The two women were picked up from the floor, shaken apart, shaken again, bumped into chairs and told to sit still and behave themselves. They sat and wept, the Belgian Chief of Police stamped about and swore, Letord made notes in his little note-book and Hambledon went out in the garden for air or perhaps for liberty to smile without being observed. Presently the two pursuers came back, panting, and said nervously that the fugitive had in effect as it were evaporated. Their Chief looked at them and his lower jaw quivered with speech that would not come. Hambledon thought it kinder to intervene.

"The prisoner," he said carefully, "cannot, with strict regard to accuracy, be said to have escaped from the police."

The big Belgian turned a bloodshot eye upon him and uttered a whinnying sound which Hambledon took for permission to continue.

"He was, in fact," pursued Tommy, "not so much running away as blasted out of our sight by the awful explosion which took place when you, m'sieu', brought those two packets of high-explosive together. I speak seriously, m'sieu'. I was watching his face and in my opinion he had entirely forgotten even that there were police present, let alone that he was under arrest. His face turned green, his jaw dropped, his eyes showed their whites all round the pupil; I have seen it before in battle, this moment before the nerve breaks. Maurice's broke and he fled before the Judgment."

"But he has gone," said the Chief. "Also the young man who exhibited a firearm in the Terminus Cafe. Also we have not yet the murderer of the young man called Yanni the Nephew though it is true we seem to have got the gun which shot him."

Letord glanced momentarily at Hambledon and took up the part of comforter.

"These young women here," said the French detective, "they have not yet told us all they know. It may be that there is, as it were, corn there for the reaping."

The Chief of Police calmed himself and issued orders.

The house would be taken over and examined minutely for any evidence of any kind which might prove useful. Experts would be sent out to deal with it and particularly with the contents of the safe. The two women would be taken separately to the police-station and housed there separately until they could be separately interrogated. He returned himself, Hambledon and Letord to the centre of Brussels where a man may lunch.

The examination of the two young women proved to be less helpful than had been hoped. Leonie Vermaas was a dancer in Roubaix when she first met Alexandre Maurice six months earlier. She knew nothing of his private affairs but understood him to be a wine-merchant. He used to come to Roubaix to visit her; when he told her that he would be in Brussels for at least three months and probably much longer they got married and he took the bungalow at Laeken. "There we were happy, m'sieu'," said Leonie, and dabbed at her eyes with a pink silk handkerchief. "Did I concern myself with his business affairs? But, no. Why should I? I was his rest, his recreation——"

Pressed for details about their marriage she became evasive, haughty and uncertain in rotation and finally admitted that they were going to be married the following week. "But now you have driven him away what shall I do?"

The Chief of Police recommended a return to Roubaix. "There, madame, he will know where to find you." Formal details of identity and address having been noted, she was set at liberty and Colette Masurel brought in in her place. She was a good deal more informative. She had known Maurice since they were children, their parents had been neighbours in Paris. She was a little older than he, two years, not much but enough to give her that prudence and discretion which Maurice, alas, so conspicuously lacked. "It was by our parents' wish that we were betrothed, they thought I might, perhaps, successfully exert a steadying influence. I promised his poor mother I would do my best. She is dead and his father also." Apparently she had a certain amount of influence over him for however long he might be away he always returned to her with a long story about his doings. It was plain that she felt a responsibility for him but she was far too level-headed to marry him as he was. "I am a hardworking woman," she said, "I earn my living making dresses," and she named a firm of international repute. "I have worked for them now nearly twenty years, I started very young. I am known and trusted, I have my position, my good reputation. I think twice before I attach myself to one so charming but so unreliable. I am, perhaps, not romantic."

Letord interrupted to say that she was above all things wise, intelligent and kind, and that if Maurice had had the sense to marry her and settle down he would not now be in this trouble.

"Indeed he has asked me, several times, but always when he is but just clear of some scrape and either frightened or sorry. I say that if he will find an honest job and keep it for two years we will speak of this again, but he never does, and now it seems he has married that pink macaw in the bungalow——"

"Oh, no, he didn't. He wasn't so silly as all that and your remarks about her marriage certificate were too true to be pleasant."

Colette smiled faintly and gave, in response to questions, some account of Maurice as she knew him. He had been in trouble once with the police, convicted and sentenced for robbing a tobacconist's shop just after the war. For the rest the picture emerged of the petty criminal for whom a little cheating and a finger in the Black Market are more congenial than work. "I tell you this, messieurs, because I think the one chance for him now is to be caught and given a lesson. If he goes on like this, and still gets away with it——"

She made a helpless little gesture and the men nodded. "If you do catch him, messieurs, may I be informed?"

"But certainly," said Letord. "At once, that is my promise."

When she had gone they looked at each other.

"Sidelight on a spiv," said Hambledon. "Why does he always go back to her?"

"The everlasting small boy," said the Belgian, "even a very horrid small boy. She is home and nursery; slaps, but security."

"I hope for her sake," said Letord, "that he does not go back once too often. He is a bad type, that one, and she knows too much about him."

X

BURENNE

HAMBLEDON and Letord were delayed in Brussels for two days while police enquiries were proceeding, they arrived in Paris in the evening of the 3rd day and their first call was at the Sûreté. Letord sent his fingerprint records to the appropriate department for identification; Yanni the Nephew's on the photographic plate and Jules Parisot's on the print of the girl which was found in his wallet. Neither of them were in the records since Yanni had never been convicted in France and Parisot had not been convicted at all. There was a short dossier about Alexandre Maurice, so far as it went it confirmed the truth of Colette Masurel's statements.

"She is truthful as well as sensible, that one," said Letord. "She is too good for him."

"She may yet be spared him," said Hambledon drily.

There was on the back of the girl's portrait the rubberstamped name and address of the photographer who took it; official enquiries identified her at once. She was Mlle. Francine Canot of The Patisserie, Boissy-le-Bel. Hambledon and Letord, with a spare policeman in case of trouble, drove out of Paris by the Charenton road, passing forests bright with autumn on their way. Boissy-le-Bel was upon no main road; the car turned and twisted through narrow

lanes inadequately signposted, acutely cornered and as to
surface completely abominable. Finally the woods closed
in upon them altogether and for the last mile they ran
through a green tunnel lit only by occasional shafts of
golden autumn sunlight striking through the trees.

"Nice now," said Hambledon appreciatively, "but a
trifle gloomy in the winter, I imagine."

"Formidable," said Letord.

They turned a corner and came suddenly upon the village one straight street running down to the river. Letord
told the driver to take it very slowly, he put the gears into
neutral and the car slid silently down the hill. There were
cottages, a butcher's shop, a general store, a small ancient
church with thick whitewashed walls and the cure's house
just behind it, more cottages and the post-office with late
roses still in the garden——

"Stop instantly," said Letord to the police driver, and
leaped out of the car before it came to rest. Hambledon
alighted less precipitately but in time to see the detective
dodge round a Marechal Niel and seize by the arm a man
who was digging a cabbage-patch behind it. The man
stuck his fork into the ground and turned; Hambledon
recognized him at once for he had seen this man follow
Yanni from the Taverne Gruber. It was Burenne.

Burenne opened his mouth and shut it again. Then his
eyes fell upon Hambledon and an expression of pleased
recognition lit up his face. This was the Englishman who
had dealt so faithfully with Maurice and been arrested for
his pains in the house in the Rue Olive. Hambledon was
puzzled, he did not think Burenne knew him and why he
should look pleased to see him was more mysterious still.

"Ah, m'sieu'——"

"Er—good afternoon," said Tommy cautiously.

Burenne looked enquiringly at him, glanced at the police, and raised his eyebrows. He was plainly asking whether Hambledon was a fellow-sufferer from the police; Tommy, completely at a loss, made a mysterious grimace and shrugged his shoulders. Burenne cast up his eyes in a gesture of resignation and Letord frankly stared.

"Burenne," he said sharply, "what are you doing here?"

"Gardening," said Burenne innocently, "for M. the postmaster, as you see."

"You gardening?" said Letord incredulously. "Tell me another. I don't believe it."

"But, m'sieu', it is true. I will be frank with m'sieu'. My past life has not, perhaps, been all that a moralist would recommend——"

"I believe that," said Letord. "I have seen your dossier."

"No doubt. I came to the conclusion that I am no longer young and that if I did not wish to deteriorate irrevocably it was time I made a change. I have, therefore, cut myself off from my previous associates and come into the country to avoid temptation. I have got myself a steady job and I propose to settle down, with your kind permission, and become a worthy citizen. I trust m'sieu' approves."

"But why here?"

Burenne sighed patiently. "Why not here? It is quiet, it is peaceful, it is remote. It is the sort of place I wanted so here I am."

"Burenne. What were you doing in Brussels last week?"

"Private business."

"Very private, I have no doubt. What was it?"

"M'sieu' will forgive me. A family matter. Is it, then, a crime to travel to Brussels?"

Letord paused. He did not wish at that stage to tax this man with the murder of Yanni-the-Nephew because he still hoped that Burenne, if left at liberty, would give the police a further lead in the matter of forged currency. Besides, it was at least curious that Burenne should be in the same village with the young woman Francine Canot who was their only link with that other young man, name as yet unknown, who had made the scene in the Taverne Gruber and immediately disappeared. It would be wisest to interrogate the girl first, one could return to Burenne later.

"Very well," said Letord, drawing back. "We will leave you to pursue the paths of righteousness. Look to it that you do not stray from them."

"A thousand thanks," said Burenne. "Believe me, I have no wish for any further contact with the police."

"You think we might find out something more about you, eh?"

"Not that, m'sieu', no. It is my reputation for which I fear—you know these villagers, so censorious—to be seen talking to the police, it is not good."

Letord told him to go to the devil and turned away laughing. Hambledon made to follow him but Burenne stayed him with a gesture.

"M'sieu' 'Armbeeldon——"

"How d'you know my name?"

"On the pad in that Rue Olive house. Are you in trouble?" Burenne jerked his head in the direction of the police.

"No, thank you. You were looking in at the window, of course. No, that was a mistake. Why?"

"I owe you something for downing that swine Maurice, that's all. Now he's safe in jail——"

"He's not," whispered Tommy. "He escaped. We are looking for him."

"Why didn't you shoot him while you'd got him?" demanded Burenne, but Hambledon left him to rejoin the car.

"To the Bakery, wherever it is," said Letord to the police driver. "What was all that, if it is not confidential?"

"My curiosity," said Tommy. "I wanted to know where he'd seen me before. He was looking in at the same window you looked through, in the Rue Olive. He saw me holding up Maurice. He doesn't like Maurice at all, quite the reverse. Wanted to know why I didn't shoot him while I had the chance. I hope I did right, I told him Maurice had escaped. Burenne might have news of him before we do."

"Interesting, that," said Letord thoughtfully. "Yes, I see no harm in your telling him; Maurice's escape is doubtless known all over the underworld already."

"Unless he ran so fast he went straight into a canal and hasn't come up again yet."

"Heaven grant it," said Letord piously, and the car pulled up at a small shop. There was a name painted above the window which announced Alphonse Canot, *Boulanger et Patissier*.

Alphonse Canot was a thin elderly man with a drooping moustache, a melancholy expression and the splayed thumbs of the habitual kneader of dough. Letord wished him a good afternoon and asked if he might have the privilege of a word with Mademoiselle Francine Canot. The baker glanced over Letord's shoulder, saw the police car outside with a uniformed driver at the wheel, and looked more melancholy than ever.

"I have the honour of addressing——?"

"I am Antoine Letord, an officer of the Sûreté, but your daughter has nothing to fear, I only want to ask her a few questions."

The baker drooped visibly. "The police," he murmured. "at my house." Obviously, he shared Burenne's views about the discrediting effects of intercourse with the police, and Hambledon smiled. Letord was a trifle nettled.

"For the well-doer," he said, "there is nothing to alarm in a visit from the police. It is an honour to be asked to assist them."

Canot made a little helpless gesture, opened a door behind him and called his daughter. Through the open door Hambledon and Letord could see that the further room was a bakehouse; even as they looked a young man crossed the further end. He was wearing a white apron and a tall white cap and was powdered all over with flour, but both Canot's visitors recognized him at once as the young man with the revolver at the Taverne Gruber. Letord vaulted the counter, dashed into the bakehouse and seized him by the arm.

"You—I want you."

"Kind heaven," moaned Canot, and the young man turned as white as his flour. There was a rush and a swish of skirts and Francine arrived.

"What is this—what has he done?" She held the boy's free hand firmly in both hers and looked defiance at the detective. She was very like her photograph; not pretty, but clean and wholesome and plump with dimples at chin and elbows, clear blue eyes and a generous mouth. Letord looked at her and his grim expression relaxed.

"He has got into a little mischief in Brussels, mademoiselle, that is all. I want to ask him some questions. First——" addressing the boy—"what is your name?"

"P-Parisot. Jules Parisot."

"Oh. Now, Jules Parisot, tell me why you entered by the back way a restaurant called the Terminus in Brussels and menaced the proprietor with a loaded revolver——"

"Oh—oh," wailed Francine, and came round to look into the boy's face. "Jules, tell me this is not true!"

"Mademoiselle," said Letord sternly, "I myself was there and saw it. He demanded a parcel—what was in that parcel?"

"I don't know," said Parisot miserably.

"You don't know? And yet you resorted to armed violence to get it?"

"A man outside," stammered Parisot, "there was a man outside—I was down and out, I only had seven francs and I wanted to come home—he offered me five hundred francs to go in and get the parcel for him. He gave me the gun. I thought they were all crooks together so it wouldn't matter and I wanted the money to get home. I didn't hurt anybody, I didn't even fire the gun——"

"Miserable boy," said the baker, and Francine sobbed.

"I dropped the gun and ran away, somebody else fired it and the next thing I remember is being locked in a store-room. I hadn't got the parcel, I don't know what happened to it. Then a friend came and got me out and brought me home."

"Name of your friend?"

"I—I don't want to say."

"Then I will say it for you," said Letord magnificently. "His name is Burenne, is it not?"

"He won't get into trouble, will he, m'sieu'?" said Francine. "M'sieu' Burenne is so good and so kind! But, a heart of gold for this poor boy."

"Indeed!" said Letord, very surprised, for the Burenne he knew was neither good nor kind. "You know him, mademoiselle?"

"For as long as I can remember, m'sieu'. He brought Jules when he first came here, to Boissy-le-Bel that is, as a little orphan boy. He was lodged with Madame Rieviere at the Mill Cottage, she brought him up with her own. I think M'sieu' Burenne knew Jules' parents, or was related to them—I do not know, m'sieu'."

"Oh. Indeed. I see. Now, Parisot, returning to your little affair in Brussels for a moment, what was the name of the man who sent you into the cafe for the parcel?"

"I do not know, he was a——"

"Do not lie to me!" thundered Letord. "His name was Maurice, was it not?"

Parisot nodded weakly, then his knees gave way and he slid to the floor in a faint. He was energetically restored and the questioning continued.

"I make no promises," said Letord, "but if you show yourself willing to help the police by telling them everything you know, truthfully and fully, it may be that you will hear no more about this ridiculous affair in Brussels. Now then. Where did you first meet Maurice?"

Parisot told the whole story up to the point where Burenne rescued him from the Terminus store-room. Yes, he knew Maurice dealt in forged currency and Parisot had even delivered parcels for him to the house in the Rue Olive. Twice, to be exact. No, he had no idea from where Maurice got the notes. Yes, he knew it was wrong but he had no money except what Maurice gave him, and whenever Parisot showed signs of shrinking Maurice threatened to inform the police that the boy was passing forged currency "and then you know where you will go, don't you?"

"See what happens," said Letord improvingly, "when a young man permits himself to become entangled with evil companions. What the devil possessed you to start it? Boredom?"

Parisot nodded more cheerfully, the worst was now over and apparently he was not going to be arrested. "During the Occupation, m'sieu', one annoyed the Germans a little now and again. I am not of the heroes of the Resistance, but there were a few small occasions—it was exciting. Then there was the Liberation, that was exciting too, and the great victory. Then, after that, we all settle down to work again——"

"And that is not so exciting, no." Letord extracted as many details about Maurice as Parisot could supply, but it was plain that the boy knew nothing beyond what he had actually seen, which was little; and indeed it was most unlikely that Maurice would permit him the smallest knowledge beyond what was unavoidable.

"I think that is all for the moment," said Letord finally, "unless my coadjutor here has any question he thinks you can answer?"

Hambledon said there was only one. "When you and Burenne left the Terminus—by the back door—where did you go?"

Parisot's nervousness returned. "To a cafe, m'sieu'. My head ached——"

"So you had a cup of coffee to freshen you up, eh? An excellent idea. And after that?"

"We started for Paris, Burenne had a car——"

"Indeed. Then what were you doing in the Rue Olive? It leads the wrong way, surely?"

"I—I had left some things——"

"In Maurice's bungalow at Laeken, possibly?"

Letord thumped his knee. "Of course! It was you and Burenne who tied up the blonde and ransacked the place. Revenge, I suppose."

Parisot stammered out that "it was reparations, m'sieu'," and Letord laughed.

"Reparations, they are so respectable today, are they not?"

"Will there be trouble over that, m'sieu', for Burenne? I would not——"

"I am not the Belgian Police," said Letord airily, "I have enough on my plate without doing their work also. Eh, m'sieu'?"

"I agree," said Hambledon. "It was only that I was curious to know who did that."

"Tell me," said Francine, "can it be that this poor Jules has no longer anything to fear?"

"If he behaves himself, mademoiselle, in future, I think he need not fear the police. I say, the police. There are others he will do well to avoid. Maurice for example."

"But Maurice was arrested!"

"People do not always stay arrested, Parisot. Keep yourself within bounds here and do not go looking for adventure. Then perhaps she will not come looking for you, eh? We take our leave, mademoiselle. *Adieu*, Parisot, see to it that it is not *au revoir*. Canot, take care not to mislay your assistant again, he might not be so lucky next time."

A further interview with Burenne added a few more details. He said that when Parisot was missing from home Papa Canot wrote to him to tell him so. "I did not get the letter for some days, I was away from home. I went to Paris and made enquiries among those who might know; I was a day too late, the boy had gone to Brussels with Maurice. I went to Brussels, I knew how to get into touch with Maurice, but before I had time to do so I saw that ridiculous affair at the Terminus. You know the rest."

"Yes, we know the rest," said Letord quietly. "You saw Maurice being arrested so you thought it was safe to go through his house for what you could get, eh?"

"Parisot told you?"

"No," said Hambledon. "You did. The Rue Olive is not the road to Paris."

Burenne nodded. "You are wrong in one thing only. It would not have mattered whether Maurice had been at home or not, I should have gone there all the same."

"Where does he get the 'slush' from, Burenne?" asked Letord.

"I don't know," said Burenne frankly. "Name of a little blue dog, I didn't know there was so much 'slush' in all the world as he had in his safe. You have seen it, no doubt."

"We have," said Hambledon. "Most impressive."

"Formidable," said Letord. "Burenne, you are also in that racket."

"What? Passing 'slush'? No, thank you, m'sieu', I

have no desire at all to qualify for transportation, I let that stuff alone."

"Think again," said Letord.

Burenne's eyebrows drew together but he only repeated, "I tell you, I let that stuff alone."

"Do you remember," said the French detective, "going to a certain table in the Taverne Gruber in Brussels to pick up a cardboard mat with an address on it? Ah yes, I see you do. How did you know where to find it if you were not in——"

"I was told that in Paris, m'sieu'. I said just now, I made enquiries about Parisot there and was told he had gone to Brussels with Maurice. I was anxious then, I knew Maurice was working that racket and I didn't want the boy to— anyway, I asked how I could find Maurice. The man who told me said he didn't know where Maurice was living but that the instructions were passed on beer-cards on a certain table at the Gruber. So I went there the first night I arrived in Brussels and watched, I saw a man pick up a card from that table and pocket it. So then I knew which table. The next night I was later getting there than I meant to be, there was a man sitting there when I arrived. I waited about till he left; you understand, m'sieu', whatever was on the card would lead me to Maurice in the end. But the man took the card away with him so I followed him to take it from him." Burenne paused and laughed awkwardly. "It wasn't so simple as that after all. I followed him up the Rue de Brabant as far as the new railway bridge, put my gun in his ribs—it had the safety-catch on —and told him to go into one of those empty spaces there. Not a good idea, I might have been had up for murder. When we got inside he whipped round like an eel, grabbed my hand with the gun in it and tried to push it up above his head, you know the trick, m'sieu' Letord. The next move is a kick in the stomach and you've had it. But the safety-catch on that automatic is defective, he squeezed my hand and the gun went off when it was level with his head, he got it between the eyes. It took me so aback I dropped the gun and before I could find it somebody came to the doorway and shouted something so I left everything and bolted. I got clear away, but I had the wind up, my fingerprints were on that gun, must have been. However, later the same evening I saw Parisot making a fool of himself at the Terminus and you know the rest. You may believe me, m'sieu', it is the truth."

Letord looked at Hambledon and laughed.

"You find it amusing," said Burenne in an angry voice. "It is true I can't prove it, but——"

"But I can," said Hambledon. "I was the man who came to the entrance to that vault and shouted at you."

"You, m'sieu'!"

"Yes. I had followed you from the Gruber, I saw the whole performance. I'd been watching Yanni pocket the card and wondered why, and I saw you come running across the square—you nearly got run over by a bus——"

"Yes, that is so, I——"

"So when you followed him I followed you. I did not tell you, Letord, but when I picked up that automatic the safety-catch was on. I jumped to the conclusion that either Burenne had pushed it on after firing——"

"No, m'sieu'——"

"Or I might even have done so myself from habit,

without realizing it. I never thought of it again until this moment."

"M'sieu'," said Burenne with some emotion, "you are without doubt my good angel. I wish I were a better man to deserve your good offices. When I saw you through the window of that house in the Rue Olive something told me——"

"Oh, put a sock in it," said Hambledon. "Well, Letord, what's the verdict? "Not guilty, but don't do it again'?"

"Let it be a lesson to you, Burenne, never to commit a murder without having an Englishman handy to prove that you didn't do it."

Upon that friendly note they parted, Hambledon and the French detective strolling down the pleasant street towards the inn. Below them the ancient bridge across the river lay in shadow for the sun was setting; the dusk crept out of the forest and joined with the blue wood-smoke from cottage chimneys in thin drifts along the valley. Beyond the river the hillside rose steeply, clothed in timber to the skyline, where the topmost branches of the tallest trees were still golden in the last sunlight. Hambledon, a countryman by birth and preference, slowed down the better to appreciate it and Letord looked round with mild surprise.

"Nice place, this," murmured Hambledon.

"Ah. M'sieu' restores himself with the beauties of Nature. Myself I feel a need of more material restoration. I am hungry. And you also?"

"Now you mention it," admitted Tommy. "Perhaps that is why I was feeling pensive. I wonder whether the inn could do something to help us?"

"Food of a horror to revolt the stomach," said Letord crisply. "We shall be back in Paris in less than an hour, where they understand how to serve a meal. Can you endure so long?"

But when they reached the inn yard where the car awaited them they found the police driver in his shirt-sleeves delving into the open bonnet while an ancient with a long white beard leaned on a stick and gave him good advice.

"Trouble, Dupont?"

"The ignition," said the driver bitterly, "again. The spare parts one is fobbed off with these days——"

"How long?"

"Anything from ten minutes to two hours. I regret. I do my utmost."

Letord sighed, Hambledon took him by the elbow and steered him into the inn. To their surprised pleasure the place was clean and bright, they were welcomed to a cheerful fire and a meal that was more than passable, it was good. There was also a wine almost commendable. When they had finished Letord went out to see how the repairs were progressing, and returned laughing.

"The ancient is holding a hurricane lantern," he said, "in one hand and his beard away with the other. I think he has lost some of it over the lamp. Dupont thinks he knows now what the trouble is and is taking down the distributor. He says another hour. I think he has been weeping. This is a nice fire, is it not?"

"I shouldn't mind staying here the night," said Hambledon, yawning.

"We may have to, yet. We'll give him a little longer. As he says, these spare parts——"

Soon after eleven Dupont came in to say that he had effected the repair and tested the car which was now running perfectly. Was it desired to start for Paris at once?

Hambledon woke up and said that so far as he was concerned the answer was negative, and shook Letord who also woke up and said that eight o'clock in the morning would do just as well. The innkeeper could accommodate them all. Dupont smiled for the first time for two hours and retired to the inn kitchen for a meal while Hambledon and Letord stumbled sleepily upstairs to bed and peace settled upon the Three Crowns.

Four hours later, at three o'clock on a misty morning Hambledon awoke with a start and listened. The sound came again, a woman's scream and someone shouting for help, help! He tumbled out of bed and into the passage where he met Letord in his inadequate underwear.

"What's all that? Murder?"

Letord snatched a coat from the door and struggled into it as he ran down the stairs. Outside in the street, fifty yards up the hill and on the further side of the road, a car engine roared into life and they saw the vehicle move off, accelerate, and disappear rapidly up the hill and out of sight.

"It's at the bakery," said Hambledon, and ran up the street to meet a sobbing white figure, Francine.

"Jules, it is Jules. They have kidnapped him."

XI

THE ROAD TO PARIS

AS in the story of La Belle au Bois Dormante the palace awakens instantly when the Prince kisses the Princess, so the one street of Boissy-le-Bel when criminals abducted the foundling boy from the bakery. Doors opened and men and women rushed out most inadequately clad; dogs barked, children screamed, and the five geese at the mill joined in the general clamour. Letord rushed into the bakery to make sure that the story was true and Hambledon followed conveying Francine, who was near to collapse. As they reached the doorway there came flying footsteps down the street and Burenne arrived at the moment when Letord came out again saying that it was true. "Where's that fool Dupont? I want the car instantly."

"I expect he's still asleep," began Hambledon, but Burenne said he would take the message. He burst through the people and ran to the inn.

"Did you see the men?" asked Letord.

"I did," said the baker. "Three of them, the bad apache type."

"Did you know any of them?"

Papa Canot called Heaven to witness that he did not number men of that type among his acquaintances. Jules,

148

however, had called one of them by name, Maurice. "No, Maurice, no!" Letord looked at Hambledon who had by now transferred Francine to her father for support, and Tommy made a grimace in reply. The motive was obvious; Maurice thought that Parisot would talk to the police and did not know that he was too late to prevent it.

"Where the hell is Dupont with the car—ah, here it comes."

The car came out of the inn yard and turned towards them, the village people scuttled out of its way, Letord and Hambledon stepped forward to meet it, but the car did not stop. Furiously driven, it passed them and flashed up the street, round the turn to Paris at the top of the hill and out of sight.

"Burenne," said Letord, breathing heavily, "Burenne was driving that car. When I catch him I will—I will——"

"Is there another car in the village?" asked Hambledon of the company in general, who replied that there was, indeed, the small Fiat saloon of M. Burenne, there was no other.

"It is in one of my sheds," said the baker, and abandoned Francine in order to lead the way. The Fiat was, in fact, the same car that Burenne had driven from Brussels; Hambledon and Letord looked at it with an emotion almost too deep for words. As was proclaimed by a small pool on the floor, the radiator leaked; the windscreen was blotched over a large part of its area. The bonnet was tied down with rope, the tyres were smooth and showing canvas in streaks, and most of the paint was missing. At this unhappy moment Dupont, the police driver, came running.

"Miserable," said Letord, addressing him. "You see that car? You will now drive it to Paris. Get on."

"But ours——"

"Stolen while you snored. *Get on*!"

Dupont looked in the tank by the light of an electric torch and said that the thing did at least contain petrol. He switched on the ignition, found that the starter did not work, and produced the starting-handle. At this point he paused and enquired in a slightly mutinous tone whether this accumulation of wreckage had actually proceeded within the last five years. When the baker said that Mr. Burenne had driven it from Brussels three days earlier Dupont blinked and wound the starting-handle angrily. The Fiat engine started at once.

"Incredible," said Letord and leapt into one front seat as Dupont climbed into the other. Hambledon got into the back and then found that the door would not remain shut.

"He had it tied with string when he came," said the baker, helping Hambledon to slam it. "He said it needed a little adjustment——"

But Dupont, muttering to himself, drove out of the yard and away. It soon became plain that there was very little the matter with the engine however dishevelled the body might be, and they made good time up the hill and bucketed down the twisting lanes.

"I begin to believe," said Letord in a surprised voice, "that it may possibly be true that Burenne drove this car from Brussels."

Hambledon did not answer, he was too busy holding the door handle with one hand and trying with the other to keep his overcoat wrapped round his naked shins;

Dupont appeared to be praying for the tyres. Ten minutes later, some half-mile from the point where the lane debouched upon the main Charenton road, a white figure dropped from the bank at the roadside ahead of them and waved its arms. Dupont applied the brakes with such care that they overshot the figure and it came running after them; Letord, however, had recognized it.

"The Parisot boy in his nightshirt. We shall now, perhaps, hear something." He opened the door and got out.

"Quick, quick!" gasped Parisot, "perhaps he is not dead. Round the next bend." He pushed Letord back into his seat and crouched on the running-board, clinging to the car.

"Drive on carefully," said Letord to the driver. "Parisot, what is all this——"

"They took me away in a car and he came up in a car behind, firing at their car, then we stopped and so did he and they all got out and he told me to run so I ran back here——"

The Fiat rounded the bend, there was a saloon car stopped at the side of the road.

"That's their car, the other one's gone, I heard it drive away——"

"There is petrol," said Dupont, "all over the road." He switched off the Fiat's engine and braked with even more care than before. There were, indeed, trails of spilt liquid upon the road and a pool at the back of the saloon; their noses told them that it was petrol. Letord got out and Parisot backed behind the Fiat.

"Perhaps they have not all gone——"

"Dupont," said Letord. "With me."

The two policemen advanced steadily upon the saloon,

clear in the Fiat's headlamps, and Letord challenged but received no reply. Hambledon got out of the back seat and Parisot shot in like a rabbit into its home burrow. There was no one in the saloon but there was a trail of blood leading from it to a point half-way across the road.

"Somebody was hit," said Letord, turning his torch upon this. "A car has stopped here, ours, no doubt. He got in and was driven away."

"The petrol tank has been hit twice," said Hambledon, "pretty shooting. Did he get that near back tyre too— he did. Lucky, very lucky. No wonder they stopped. But where is Burenne now?"

"Perhaps Parisot can tell us some more," said Letord, and led the way back to the Fiat.

Parisot said that when the saloon stopped Burenne also pulled up. He was behind the police car when he shouted to Jules to run, he was firing from behind it.

"How many shots did he fire?"

Parisot said six or seven times before they stopped and twice afterwards.

"Two guns," said Hambledon. "And then he ran out of ammunition. He wouldn't have time to reload, I expect they rushed him."

"There was my revolver in the cubby-hole in the dash," said Letord. "Where did Burenne stop, Parisot? Here? Yes, I see the marks. Any blood about?"

But there was not, and no sign of Burenne.

"Either they took him with them, dead or alive," said Letord, "or he went over the bank and across the fields here."

"Leaving Parisot in his little nightgown all alone?" said

Hambledon. "Well, he might if he had some urgent errand."

"Such as getting away from us," suggested Letord. "He would see our headlights coming."

"Or just getting away from Maurice and Company," said Hambledon, shivering. "What do we do now?"

"Back to Boissy-le-Bel," said Letord. "We can do no more here at present. Dupont, you will remain beside the saloon here until you are relieved. You are at least wearing trousers which is more than we are. What is that rattling noise?"

"Parisot's teeth chattering," said Tommy, "or is it mine? Talking of trousers brings it home to me what I'm suffering."

Letord backed the Fiat into a gateway, turned, and drove back to Boissy-le-Bel.

"What I want to know," said Hambledon, sitting beside Letord in front, "is how Maurice knew that Parisot had come home. The last Maurice saw was Parisot knocked out in the Terminus and police arriving from all angles."

"Ask him," said Letord with a jerk of his head towards the back seat. Hambledon turned to Parisot and repeated his question.

"I exp-p-pect somebody in P-paris t-told him," stammered the boy. "We stopped in P-paris c-coming through and Burenne s-saw some of his friends. We—we d-didn't know that M-maurice was loose again." His teeth chattered so uncontrollably that he could hardly speak.

"Burenne may have told somebody about Maurice's bungalow at Laeken," said Letord thoughtfully. "All that 'slush', you know. Too good to keep dark, especially i Maurice was in jail."

"Yes. Is Maurice going round exterminating everyone who is likely to give information about him? Rather a large order, perhaps."

"I wish he would," said Letord, laughing. "It would clean up the underwold of Paris for us to a marvel."

Hambledon thought of Colette and raised his eyebrows, but as Letord was plainly not thinking about her it seemed pointless to remind him. They returned the shivering Parisot to the care of Francine and had a few quiet words with her father.

"Burenne is curiously interested in that boy's welfare," said Hambledon. "There must be a reason."

"There is," said the baker, "but it is not generally known. Between gentlemen and in confidence, Jules is his son. Burenne and I, we have known each other all our lives, our parents lived in the same street when we were children. We fought in the 1914 war. He married, she was a bad type, that one. She left him when Jules was a baby not old enough to speak plain. He—Burenne, I would say—he fell among bad companions and got into trouble, I never asked, it was no business of mine. He came to see me sometimes. I married a girl of Boissy-le-Bel and came here to live. We bought this business, we were not rich, I borrowed the money. Then my creditor wished to be repaid, he demanded it. By this time Burenne had put the little Jules with a woman of this village. I told him of our difficulties and he—my friend—paid the debt. I have repaid him a little, not much. He said that when Jules was old enough he should come to me and learn to be a baker, that would repay him enough. He is anxious about Jules, that he should not go the same way, you understand? When he learned that Jules had gone with that gang he went almost mad, so he told me. He brought Jules back and said that he, Burenne, would take a job here and settle down, it was time, he said. He would take up gardening, he liked it."

"He told me that," said Letord. "I did not believe him."

"It was quite true, m'sieu'. He was well brought up, you understand, it was natural that he should wish to become respectable at the last. And that Jules should be, that is why it was a secret that he was Jules' father, in case he should at any time become notorious."

"A curious story," said Hambledon.

"But true, m'sieu'."

"I believe you. Eh, Letord?"

"I think it is probably true," said Letord. "I fear, though, that he has left his reformation rather late."

The baker looked mournfully at the detective. "You mean that you know more about his doings than I do. I feared much, but I never asked, I do not wish to know. In any case it does not matter. I expect he is already dead."

"He might have got away across the fields," said Hambledon, but Canot would not be comforted.

"He was not a good man, gentlemen, but he was a good friend to me. They will not let him live, those others. No."

When Hambledon and Letord returned to Paris the following morning they were told that the police car which Burenne had driven away had been found. It was on the Sûreté's very own car park. Carefully examined, it showed blood smears on the leather upholstery, but since it was known already that one of Maurice's party had been hit the discovery told them nothing about Burenne's fate. The saloon car which had been left, ditched, after Burenne had disabled it, proved to have been stolen in Paris the night before. It belonged to a perfectly respectable doctor who wanted to know how he was supposed to attend to his practice if the police allowed his car to be taken away by brigands and wrecked. It did provide one good thumb print of a gentleman known as Toto the Giraffe who specialized in larceny from the person with or without violence.

"Bring me," said Letord, "the miserable carcases of Alexandre Maurice and Toto the Giraffe, dead or alive. Also the man Burenne, alive if possible."

His subordinates saluted alertly and hurried away and Hambledon said that, precisely speaking, carcases were always dead, were they not?

"Does it matter?" asked Letord, busily going through reports which told him nothing that he wanted to know.

"I was wondering whether Colette Masurel has seen anything of Maurice since he returned."

"For her sake I hope not, but it is possible. She will be at her place of business still," said Letord, glancing at the clock. "I could send someone to interview her."

"One of your men?" said Hambledon in a doubtful voice.

"You are thinking it might cause comment among the staff, are you not? We cannot afford to consider that when it is a question of arresting criminals."

"Of course not. How would it be if I were to go? I can make it obvious that I am English."

"But, certainly. The very thing. Get someone to show you the staff entrance, you will catch her when she comes out."

Hambledon provided himself with a dozen expensive

carnations in pink tissue paper and presented himself at the staff entrance of the famous establishment where Colette had worked so long. Presently the staff came flowing out, chattering and clattering along the pavement in their exaggerated shoes; Hambledon got in the way, apologized in English and French and looked embarrassed.

"Is it possible to be of assistance to m'sieu'?"

"Oh—er—a thousand thanks—I was hoping to meet someone and I was told she would come out this way, I'm frightfully sorry——"

"If m'sieu' would care to entrust us with the lady's name——"

"Mademoiselle Colette Masurel."

"Oh—ah! But, certainly. Mademoiselle Masurel will be one of the last to come out, she is one of the heads of departments, you understand."

"No doubt m'sieu' knows that already, Marie!"

"If m'sieu' would care to wait just inside, someone could run up with a message——"

"On no account," said Hambledon firmly. "I have no wish to hurry Mademoiselle Masurel. If there is a corner where I should be less in everybody's way——"

He was conducted politely to a glass cell just inside the door normally inhabited by a porter now busy locking up doors, connecting burglar and fire alarms and generally putting the house to bed. The escort of girls ran off giggling.

"The Masurel has made a conquest at last!"

"An Englishman, and rich! Observe his beautiful brown shoes!"

"And the flowers. Carnations, Marie——"

Presently Colette Masurel came along the passage, walking gracefully, dressed all in black as Frenchwomen know how to dress. Tommy stepped forward, swept off his hat and offered her the carnations. She stopped abruptly.

"Mademoiselle remembers me? We met in Brussels."

"But, of course. You were—has anything happened?"

"I have a little news, yes, and wondered whether you had more. If you would graciously accept these few vegetables, people will be sure I am not the police."

"Vegetables!" Colette broke into a laugh. "But how kind, how thoughtful you are! How did you guess that I love best carnations?" she added, for the benefit of such girls as were within earshot and elaborately pretending that they were not interested. "The scent, the colour! Shall we walk a little way? These back-door surroundings are not inspiring."

They strolled together along the street, Colette making much of the flowers.

"I was hoping you might be persuaded to dine with me at some restaurant, mademoiselle, if you have no other engagement."

"Enchanted, m'sieu'."

They dined together at a restaurant overlooking the Tuileries Gardens and Hambledon told her of Maurice's doings at Boissy-le-Bel the night before. He made light of the story but she turned pale as she listened.

"This Burenne—who is he? And Pari—, what is his name? I do not know any of these people."

"I think there is perhaps little harm done. The Parisot boy is back in his bakery with his future papa-in-law to look after him, and Burenne is more than capable of looking after himself. All the same, I think that what you said in Brussels about Maurice is true, it is time he was caught and given a lesson. If he goes on like this he may do something really serious. You have no idea where he is?"

She shook her head. "None, m'sieu'. I did not even know, until you told me, that he was in Paris."

The search for Maurice and his associates continued throughout the next day without effect; even Toto the Giraffe, conspicuous by his ridiculously long neck, was not seen in any place to which the eyes of the police were admitted. Nor was Burenne in evidence.

"Paris," said Letord thoughtfully, "is without doubt the finest city the world contains, but it is not well adapted for the apprehension of criminals. Moreover, these are men of the type about whom their acquaintances do not gossip. They discourage it."

"Cheer up," said Tommy Hambledon. "They will not evade you for ever. Any news from Brussels?"

"The fluffy-haired girl Leonie, the alleged Madame Maurice, has left for Roubaix. She said she was going there to find a flat and the bungalow is shut for the present."

"Oh? And has she actually arrived at Roubaix?"

"No business of mine," said Letord.

"Unless she comes to Paris," suggested Hambledon. "To join darling Maurice, you know. I think you might then behold Maurice in the act of departing somewhere else. A bold man, but not with women. You should have seen him shrinking from Brigitte. Well, I don't think my remarks are really helpful, I'll remove the inconvenience as they say in Spain—or is it Italy? I'll see you in the morning, Letord."

But he had not quite reached his hotel when a police car

pulled in beside the pavement at his elbow and Letord leaped out.

"There is news. They have found Burenne."

"What? Where?"

"At Colette Masurel's flat. He is dead."

"And what about Colette?" asked Hambledon, pushing Letord back into the car and climbing in after him.

"There is a dead woman there also," said Letord heavily, "but my police do not know Colette. It may not be her."

"May not," said Hambledon.

XII

CARNATIONS FOR COLETTE

COLETTE MASUREL lived on the second floor of a fairly modern block of small flats. There was an electric lift which users had to work themselves since there was no porter; there was a staircase which wound round the lift in the usual manner; there were two front doors facing each other on the ground floor and also upon each of the five floors above. There were police upon the ground floor, the first and the second, principally employed in pushing people back into their flats every time they opened their doors and tried to come out. There was a gentleman upon the first floor who desired to keep an important engagement.

"I regret," said the police officer. "It is forbidden for anyone to leave at present. A murder has been committed and a statement will be required."

"But my engagement——"

"I regret. A statement will be required."

"I will return within the half-hour——"

"I regret. It is forbidden."

The gentleman tore his hair and the officer asked if he could not telephone his friends.

"She—they are not on the telephone. I will take a taxi——"

"I regret. A murder has been committed and a statement will be required."

Colette's door was open because it was at the moment impossible to shut it. Burenne was lying face downwards just inside the door with his legs sprawling across the threshold, he had a revolver in his right hand and was quite dead. Colette was lying against a sofa at the far end of the room in an attitude which suggested that she had fallen upon it and slid from it to the floor. She had been shot through the forehead and had plainly been killed instantly. By her side on the floor was a small automatic close to her right hand. Hambledon, hat in hand, looked from one to the other while Letord questioned the two police officers in the room. The smell of powder still hung in the air and mingled with the scent of Hambledon's carnations in a tall vase on the bureau.

Letord turned to Hambledon and said: "Nothing has been touched and the photographer will be here in a moment. What do you think happened here?"

"Burenne moved after he fell, look. She did not, obviously. Therefore, it would seem that she shot him first and that he managed to shoot her before he died. But why? She told me she did not know him and I am sure that she was telling the truth. Did anyone hear when he came? How long was that before the shooting started? He was standing in the doorway with the door open, had he just arrived or was he just going?"

"All these questions must be asked," said Letord. "There is this, my friend. She told you she did not know Burenne; that is, she did not know the name. She might have known the man. Otherwise it is inconceivable that she should shoot a total stranger as he entered the room, it does not make sense. We will see what the neighbours have to tell us, unfortunately the flat opposite is untenanted at the moment, the people are away, but those above and below may know when he came. Somebody," said Letord savagely, "has got to have seen him come. As to why he did it; he was at war with Maurice, this is a piece of vengeance."

"Yes," said Hambledon slowly, "yes, that is the story which this scene conveys."

"You do not believe it?"

"I should want to be convinced that the bullets which killed them were actually fired from those two guns."

"Naturally, that must be proved. You are experienced, my friend, can you see anything to contradict the story? Before, of course, we begin to examine the affair properly. Where is this photographer? I wish to start the investigation."

"I don't see anything obvious which suggests any other explanation, though, as you say, you have not started yet. It's only that I just don't believe it. It's wrong somewhere, Letord. Psychologically wrong, more, it's ridiculous. These two people would not have done this."

"Burenne you hardly knew," said Letord, "and you liked the woman Masurel. Burenne was not always the good papa to his motherless boy, I will show you his dossier."

"Here is your photographer," said Hambledon, glad to have the discussion interrupted since he had no evidence to support his view and Letord plainly did not share it.

The photographer came and set about his business, the police surgeon came and told them no more than they knew already; then the *Juge d'Instruction* came, the magistrate whose business it is to conduct the preliminary examination and interrogate the immediate and obvious witnesses. The tenants of adjacent flats were herded together into a room on the ground floor and questioned in the presence of each other, as is the French custom. They had very little to say that was helpful. The tenants above and below heard the shots and agreed that the interval between them was short, a matter of seconds, five or ten seconds. Nobody had seen Burenne arrive. People came to the block of flats in the course of the evening, naturally, but as Colette lived upon the second floor and there were three more floors above, it was quite impossible for the ground- and first-floor tenants to tell whether the visitors were for Colette's flat or for those above hers. They heard the whine of the lift at intervals, certainly, if one can truly be said to hear a sound so constantly recurrent that one ceases at last to observe it at all. One woman said frankly that she would be more likely to notice it if it did not run for a space of time. Besides, there were the stairs, he might have walked up. It was unfortunate in the extreme that the tenants of the flat opposite Colette's should happen to be away from home. Hambledon sat in a corner behind the magistrate and said nothing. When it was all over he and Letord returned to the flat, the bodies had been removed and Letord, with a sigh of relief, shut the front door.

"Now," he said, "we begin."

There was a police officer still in the flat, the three men began by walking all about it. The front door opened straight into the sitting-room, a large pleasant room with two windows and a door at the further end which led to a short passage. On one side of this was

Colette's bedroom, very neat and tidy, and a bathroom; on the other a small spare bedroom under dustsheets, not in use, and a kitchen. There was a further door beside the kitchen window and Hambledon opened it.

"Fire-escape," he said. Letord came to look over his shoulder at the openwork iron staircase which zig-zagged up to the floors above and down to the ground. On each floor there was a gallery which ran across the building to connect with the second flat.

"Smeary," said Hambledon, turning an electric torch on the handrail. "Smuts wiped off, look."

"Someone has been down that stair recently," agreed Letord.

"Window-cleaner," said the attendant police officer. "This is his day."

"How do you know?"

"I enquired."

Letord gave him a nod of approval and then another idea occurred to him.

"Did you unlock that door, my friend?"

"No," said Tommy, "no. It was not locked."

"Did you, Durand? No? That is curious, but there may be some simple explanation. Let us go in again."

They searched the flat thoroughly; it did not take long since Colette was not of those who hoard trifles. Within the bureau they made their one helpful discovery, a letter which had been hastily dropped into a drawer.

" 'Very dear Colette,' " read Letord. " 'You are in great danger. You were seen talking to someone connected with the police and the gang are after you. I am coming to look after you, I will come tonight as soon as I can. Till then, be careful. Get your gun ready, these men are dangerous. Fear not, I will come.' It is signed A.M.," added Letord. "This clears the ground, does it not? This is Maurice, if he came at all he was too late. He looks into the hall below there and sees police everywhere. What does he do? He goes away again, naturally. You agree?"

"It looks like that," said Hambledon. "This gang of which he speaks, what is it?"

"How do I know? Burenne doubtless had associates."

"What did she know about Burenne's associates? Did he work with a gang?"

Letord hesitated and then said frankly that Burenne had the reputation of working alone. "But he may have joined a gang for some enterprise——"

"When he had just decided to retire?"

"You believe that? Can the Ethiopian change his skin? Me, I do not believe it. You are hard to convince in this matter."

"I am convinced of one thing," said Hambledon harshly. "She was killed because I took her out to dinner last night. I believe that part of Maurice's letter, at least. I have been in Paris with you four days, have I not? What has some gang of which I never heard to fear from a man who has only been in Paris four days? Besides, Burenne thought himself rather a friend of mine, he approved of my hunting Maurice. Why should he kill her, then, for talking to me?"

"He killed her, in my opinion, to be revenged on Maurice," said Letord.

"Having first warned him that he was going to do so?"

"He might."

"Very well, he might. What does Maurice do? Does

he ring her up at her place of business and tell her not to go home tonight on any account but to go and stay the night with a friend? No. He sends her a letter addressed here for her to find when she comes in, telling her to stay here till he comes. When did those witnesses hear the shots? At ten minutes past twenty-three hours, yes. She comes home from work at about nineteen hours. For four hours, therefore, she sits here alone with her little automatic for company, waiting for the bell to ring. Or are you telling me she did not even lock the front door? You have a precedent, it is true, apparently she did not lock the fire-escape door either, but perhaps that was an oversight. What does she do all those four hours? I gave her a telephone number by which she could get in touch with me, she does not use it. She sits here and waits for two men to come; one to kill her, the other to protect her. Are you telling me that she had no means of knowing which was which before she opened that door? It is an electric bell, one can signal with it. Two longs and a short, for example. Maurice had been her fiancee for years, are you telling me that he did not ring in a manner she could always recognize? Or why not speak to him through the letter-box? Then a man comes and she opens the door. Is it Maurice, who has left her in great danger alone for four hours before he troubles to turn up? No, it is Burenne, whom I still believe she did not know, for I described him to her. She doesn't wait for him to say he has come to the wrong flat or has a message for her, she shoots a total stranger on sight. Well, after——"

"A total stranger with a gun in his hand," said Letord. "Perhaps she did speak to him through the letter-box. Perhaps he said he had a message from Maurice. She would open it then, would she not? Gun in hand, of course, just in case. As for Maurice not coming in time, we do not know what has happened. He may have been run over in the street on his way here."

"If he has," said Hambledon, "I will make a special journey to the Morgue to apologize to him. But——"

"You are still not satisfied," said Letord. "My friend, I have the greatest respect for your powers of deduction and your reputation endorses my opinion. If you can produce one, just one little bit of evidence to suggest that this affair here is other than it seems, I will go into it with all my resources. My weak point is the motive, I see that for myself, but Maurice caught Burenne the night before last and who knows what cause for reprisals was given before Burenne escaped? Evidence, all I ask is evidence and all I have says that Burenne came here and shot her. Well?"

"I give up," said Hambledon. "The only suggestion I can make is that if any of the finger-prints you have been so carefully photographing turn out to be Maurice's——"

"You think he did come, do you?"

"I don't know what I think, and that's the truth. I just feel there is something wrong here, that's all."

But no finger-print identifiable as Maurice's was found in the flat. Further, the ballistics experts proved that the bullet which killed Colette came from the gun in Burenne's hand, and that which killed Burenne was fired from Colette's automatic.

"I was wrong, that's all," said Hambledon.

The days passed and nothing fresh came to light. There came a report from Lyons of a quantity of forged currency notes in circulation in that district; Letord went there and came back with some samples which experts declared to have been made, almost certainly, by the same printing press as those captured in Brussels.

"I have seen notes like this before," said the man from the *Hotel de la Monnaie*—the French Mint. "During the War—and even after—they were made at the concentration camp at Sachsenhausen. Certain prisoners were assembled there whose lawful pre-war trade had been the making and printing of currency notes. They were given all the plant they required and certain privileges—even luxuries—to encourage them. They turned out notes so good that the ordinary bank-teller could not detect them. Only men specially trained for the purpose."

"Indeed," said Hambledon. "Sachsenhausen is in the Russian zone if I remember correctly."

"M'sieu' is, indeed, accurate in his geography."

"And these days in which we live are still 'after the War' are they not?"

The Frenchmen shrugged their shoulders and Hambledon went out for a walk. This case, which had refused for so long in Brussels to admit even the smallest ray of light and had then suddenly exploded into life, appeared to have closed down again completely. Tommy was getting fidgety. Colette and Burenne had shot each other, obviously, and his strong feeling that the picture was bogus received no support from the evidence. Maurice and supporting caste had faded from the scene and might now be anywhere on the continent of Europe; Parisot was undisturbed in his bread-making at Boissy-le-Bel. There came a nip in the air at night and morning of the sunny autumn days and nothing whatever happened to help the investigation in the slightest. It is a measure of

Hambledon's irritated disquiet that he took to going for long walks about Paris, dropping into small shops for unimportant purchases and into undistinguished *Bistrots* for a drink and to talk to anyone who was willing to talk to him. Plenty of people talked but no one said anything helpful. No one even tried to pass him a forged note.

At last, upon one of these undirected prowls, he turned into a street of which he never learned the name; a narrow street, half warehouse and half slum. The evening was at that point when though the lamps are lit they throw no beams and the scene was obscure without being dark. Hambledon strolled along the pavement, there were few people about and little traffic; ahead of him a car with its back towards him was drawn in to the kerb at the mouth of an alley. When he was almost abreast of it there was a sound of scuffling in the alley and three men came out bringing with them by force a fourth man who was resisting violently. Hambledon drew back into a doorway and then saw to his astonishment that the fourth man was Maurice, he whom apparently everyone wanted. The three abductors were certainly not police and they were not being gentle, Maurice yelled for help at the top of his voice.

Hambledon attacked at once, whoever these thugs were they should not have Maurice. The sudden onslaught took them by surprise, Tommy snatched Maurice from them and hit him hard on the point of the chin, thinking even as he did so that Brigitte's stewpan would be welcome here. Maurice bent at the knees and collapsed on the pavement; the three men paused momentarily, uncertain whether Hambledon was with them or against them. In the short silence there came shouts of

"Police! Assassins!" along the street, doors opened and people rushed out.

"My bird, gentlemen," said Hambledon, hoping to detain the party till help arrived. "Who are you?" But they turned to scramble into the car and he was so ill-advised as to attempt to detain them. There followed a short and confused brawl at the end of which Hambledon, having refused to let go, was dragged into the car and driven away, leaving Maurice inert upon the pavement.

The police arrived, drawn by the sound of tumult, and recognized Maurice with delight. Here was something for which they had been looking, but what was the rest of the story? The people gathered in the street told their tale with many discrepancies, but it was made plain that some man had been taken away in a big saloon car. No, they did not know what any of the men looked like, nor what the car's number was, but there was a lady driving.

"A lady?"

With fair hair and a fur coat-collar turned up about her ears, one could not see her face. No one knew how the fight started. The police removed Maurice, who was still giving no trouble, and the street simmered down gradually into peace.

Hambledon was not missed that night; he was his own master and went wherever he liked. It was not until Letord's letters were laid before him next morning that there was any disquiet. One of the letters, typed upon cheap paper, was addressed to Letord personally.

"You have Maurice," it began abruptly, "we have the English Monsieur Hambledon. We propose an exchange. We want Maurice. Let not your official conscience be troubled; he will die as he deserves for the murder of

Mlle. Colette Masurel and Louis Burenne. You do not know, but we do, that he shot them both. We do but wish to have half-an-hour's conversation with him before he dies. We wish the Englishman no harm but either we receive Maurice or——. We will not insult your intelligence by supplying the alternative.

"If you agree, be pleased to insert an advertisement in tonight's *France-Soir* to the effect that a laundress has a white cat for sale. Arrangements for effecting the exchange will immediately thereafter reach you.

"Once more, fear not, Maurice is to die."

The letter was unsigned and had been posted in Paris the night before.

Letord tore his hair for the situation was extremely awkward. Since he and Hambledon had come together upon the forged currency enquiry, the Englishman had been officially accredited to the French police as he had been to the Belgian police at the outset. There was no doubt at all which of the two men was the more valuable; what the English would say if the French police allowed Hambledon's throat to be cut in order to preserve a *vaurien* like Maurice, Letord preferred not to imagine. On the other hand, to yield to the threats of a gang of criminals was quite unthinkable. He spared a few precious minutes to curse Hambledon earnestly for having led them into this dilemma and then went to lay the problem before his superior officers.

"I warned him," said Letord. "I implored him to accept police protection if he would expose himself to danger. I told him——"

"You cannot tell the English, it is useless to try. What did he say?"

"Nothing. He laughed."

"It would be so. The good God only knows what will make the English laugh. It is, in effect, unprofitable, this discussion. It is a matter of what is to be done. This letter, will it tell us anything?"

"It might if we had two months in which to trace it," said Letord. "We can test for finger-prints as a matter of routine, but there will be none."

He was right, there were none.

"The man Maurice," said Letord. "We have at least acquired Maurice and he must know something. He will now talk, or I myself, Antoine Letord, will attend to him. Let him be brought."

When the police had picked up Maurice from the pavement the previous evening they took him to the police-station of that district and lodged him in a cell for the night. He was not badly hurt; he began to recover consciousness on the way, he was given coffee when he arrived, and a quiet night's rest completed the cure. When he awoke in the morning he had not even a headache. There had been, naturally, some telephoning overnight between authorities on the subject of the prisoner.

"I want to talk to him," said Letord. "He can throw at least some light on an enquiry upon which I have been and still am engaged."

"Which will doubtless form the subject of the charge?" said the Divisional Superintendent.

"In effect, no," said Letord, and paused. The only illicit currency dealings which they could prove against Maurice had taken place in Belgium, not France. "Charge him with the attempted kidnapping of Jules Parisot from the *patisserie* at Boissy-le-Bel. That will serve admirably to detain him and has the merit of being perfectly true."

Maurice was accordingly taken from his cell in the morning and charged with attempted kidnapping. He asked for bail which was refused, and was removed to a real prison to await trial. He was taken there in a prison van which made a tour of the police-stations of Paris collecting candidates as it went; by the time it turned in at the prison gates there were six men in various degrees of scruffy disarray besides Maurice who was clean and neat. He withdrew into a corner of the van, tidied his hair once more with a pocket comb, and waited with bright-eyed intelligence for whatever might happen.

At the jail it was visiting day, and the usual row of depressed people sat uneasily upon the usual wooden benches waiting their turn to be allowed a few words with the family black sheep. The latest prisoners were ushered in in single file with Maurice somewhere in the middle, and one by one passed the warder's desk where their particulars were noted down. The place was actually a long stone-floored corridor; the warder's desk was in an alcove on the right and the wooden benches containing visitors ran along the left-hand wall. Each prisoner came up to the desk, stopped, was as it were introduced by the police, questioned, entered up, and passed on to make room for the next. The whole line therefore waited, moved on two steps and waited again. Maurice, having passed the desk, waited while the next man was questioned and looked about him. The visitors were of all sorts and ages, but every one clutched a card which was his entry permit and had to be given up as he or she went out. There were vacant spaces upon the benches.

The line moved on again, two steps and stop. More visitors came in, an old woman leaning on the arm of a younger one. Maurice glanced back at the police escort, he was leaning over the warder's desk explaining something on the sheet. Maurice dodged round the old woman, took two quick steps across the passage and sat down on the bench opposite perfectly still, with his head down, his shoulders hunched, and the same air of patient misery as had all the other visitors. The last prisoner in his convoy was dealt with and the line moved forward through a further door out of sight. The warder stretched himself, picked up his papers and walked after them.

Maurice got up at once, walked unhurriedly along the line and began inspecting passes; just a glance and a muttered "Correct", and handed them back. The fourth visitor whom he addressed was an elderly man who was plainly what is kindly called "simple".

"Hullo, Dad, they haven't stamped yours properly."

"Wha'? Wha's that?"

"O.K. You sit tight, I'll see to it for you."

Maurice strode purposefully along the passage, with the card held loosely between his fingers, to the outer door where he gave it up to the warder on duty and straightway walked out into the street and disappeared among the traffic just in time. Only just, for beyond the door at the end of the passage counting was taking place and a checking against the list. Alexandre Maurice, missing. A warder burst out of the door and ran along the passage, had such a one passed that way? The warder on the gate admitted that certainly such a one had, with a visitor's pass, and the first warder tore his hair to the accompaniment of the old man's plaintive enquiries. "Where's my bit o' card? Where's young man wi' my bit o' card?"

When, therefore, Letord demanded the presence of Alexandre Maurice instantly, someone of high moral courage and indomitable soul had the task of explaining that this prisoner was not available. The indomitable soul eventually disengaged himself from the subsequent proceedings and was found in a distant corridor composing epitaphs for Antoine Letord.

XIII

"WHOSE GRAVES ARE SET"

LETORD'S superior officer decided that no avoidable risks should be taken with a life so valuable as that of Thomas Elphinstone Hambledon of British Intelligence. Accordingly, the advertisement of the laundress who had a white cat for sale duly appeared in the *France-Soir* in spite of the fact that the police no longer had Maurice for barter.

"By the time their impertinent instructions are received we may have regained Maurice. One thing is certain, he will not himself approach them, or even permit them to learn that he is free, if he can help it."

"It at least gives us a few days' grace," admitted Letord, "before they begin to send us samples of Hambledon to attest their resolution. An ear, for example." He left the room and addressed a gathering of plain-clothed detectives.

"You will dissect Paris, put the fragments through a mincing-machine, sieve the results and bring me this Englishman. Also the body, dead or alive but preferably the latter, of Alexandre Maurice. If you require further assistance such as the Garde Republicaine or the Chasseurs Alpins come and tell me. The only thing you are not to tell me is that you have failed to find these men. Go."

They went, but they failed to find Hambledon in Paris because he was no longer there. He travelled to the Belgian frontier, gagged and bound, in a small van illegally adorned with the insignia of the French Corps of Signals and crossed the frontier by night under the influence of drugs in a sack. He was picked up by a car a mile on the Belgian side, having been pushed along farm tracks in a wheel-barrow. When he returned to painful consciousness he was lying on the floor of a car being driven through streets. His view of the outside world was limited in the extreme, but the triumphant figure of St. Michael on his obelisk in the Place de Brouckère crossed his sight for a moment.

"I know that figure," he thought, "where is it?"

They passed down a wide street of tall houses which did not help him since he could only see the top storeys; the car stopped for traffic lights at a broad intersection. Soon after it started again there came into his view a façade which was unmistakeably familiar, besides, it wore its name in enormous letters across the attic storey. Albert I. Hambledon's own hotel in Brussels. Brussels again.

When they stopped at the gate of Maurice's bungalow at Laeken two men got out from the front of the car and one of them ran up the path to the house. The other, a skinny man with an absurdly long neck, opened the door at Hambledon's feet and looked at him.

"So you are awake," he said, not unkindly. "Pretty stiff, I expect. Never mind, it won't be for much longer."

The second man returned from the bungalow and said it was all right. Both men looked up and down the road, there was no one about nor any lights in any houses. Hambledon realized that it must be very early in the morning; the grey twilight was that of dawn and not evening, there was a clear yellow streak across the sky to the east but the day was not yet fully come, it was long before sunrise. Hambledon was cramped and aching in every limb; when the men got him out of the car and, cutting his bonds, tried to stand him on his feet, his legs gave way and they had to carry him. Returning animation gave him such pain that the perspiration was running down his face and he was almost fainting when they carried him into the sitting-room and put him into one of Leonie's big armchairs.

The first pleasurable sensation which he had experienced for twelve hours was the smell of coffee, the next was the arrival of the long-necked man, almost certainly Toto the Giraffe, with a tray. There was not only coffee, there were rolls and butter also, and Hambledon discovered that he was desperately hungry. He struggled to a sitting position with almost audible creaks in his joints and his hands went out towards the tray in a series of uncontrollable jerks.

"It is the stiffness," said Toto. "It is better that I help you."

He poured out a cup of coffee and helped Hambledon to drink it, buttered the rolls and put them within easy reach, after which he sat down on the arm of a chair opposite and produced a revolver which he held by the barrel.

"It is better perhaps if I explain," he said.

"The situation demands clarification," agreed Hambledon sourly.

"We have no wish to kill you or even to damage you in any way."

"Any further way," amended Tommy.

"As you wish. You are only to be kept here until certain negotiations are successfully completed."

Hambledon managed to attain his mouth with a buttered roll and was too busy to answer, so Toto went on:—"You will be put in a place of safety, but there is no wish to cause you avoidable discomfort. We will bring you food regularly and, if you wish, books and papers to read. There is nothing to fear so long as you give no trouble. If you do——" he gestured with the revolver as one hitting someone on the head with the butt.

"I see. Let brotherly love continue, in short. But suppose these negotiations are not successful?"

"Let us not distress ourselves with the contemplation of unpleasant possibilities," said Toto smoothly.

The rest of the meal passed in silence so far as Tommy was concerned, but the second man came in and said that the preparations were complete when the gentleman was ready.

"He may as well finish his breakfast here," said The Giraffe. "It will save us trouble."

The other nodded and leaned against the doorpost until Hambledon had urged the last drop from the coffee-pot and cleared the last crumbs from his plate. The pain in his limbs was passing but it was still an effort to move; they had to help him out of the chair and when he tried to walk he staggered. They led him, one holding each arm, into the kitchen where he saw with surprise that the electric stove was lying on its side. The kitchen floor was stone-flagged, the stove was bolted down to one of the flag-stones and normally looked quite immoveable; now it appeared that the flag-stone was hinged and came up with the stove still attached to it. There resulted a hole in the floor nearly two feet square with a fixed iron ladder within it leading downwards to a lighted room below.

Getting Hambledon down the ladder presented some difficulties but was managed at last; he found himself in a room about nine feet by seven with rough walls, a stone floor, an oil lamp hanging from a nail and one electric light in the roof. The room was furnished with a stretcher bed complete with pillow and blankets, one light chair and a rug on the floor. His jailers sat him down on the edge of the bed, saying that lunch would be brought at half-past twelve; after which they climbed up the ladder and shut the flag-stone down.

Hambledon looked dismally about him but noticed with relief that the air was fresh, there were ventilating gratings high up in one of the walls. Nor was there any sign of damp, the place must have been very soundly constructed. He sighed and lay down upon the bed, wrapping the blankets round him and covering his eyes from the light; in five minutes he was sound asleep.

Lunch arrived in due course as promised, one man came down the ladder and the other lowered the tray to him; except at the moment when they were both engaged with the tray the man at the top covered Hambledon with his revolver. It was plain that it would be quite futile to attack the man within reach even during this short interval, since the man at the top had only to drop the tray to snatch up his gun again. They did not speak, nor did Hambledon. Perhaps a time would come when one of them would be alone and some opportunity might present itself. In the meantime the food was good and cleanly if roughly served. Hambledon sat on the edge of the bed and proceeded to enjoy such small blessings as came his way. The two men watched him from above for a few minutes before shutting down the flag-stone again. This time he noticed a small thud, like a single tap with a hammer, and at the same moment the electric light went out, leaving him with only the light from the oil lamp which was anything but brilliant. He decided to protest about this when next he saw his jailers, in the meantime he took the lamp down from the wall and set it on the chair beside him. Hambledon examined the walls of his cell with close attention; not that there seemed the faintest prospect of getting out through the walls since presumably he was sitting in what was basically a hole in the ground, but there was nothing else to look at. The walls had been constructed of odd materials, largely of brick with squared stone blocks in places and even short lengths of timber here and there, all cemented into place. No doubt whoever built it had availed himself of any materials which happened to be conveniently available. Hambledon moved slowly round his prison tentatively pushing and picking at any spot which seemed less firm than the rest. One piece of wood, about three feet long and three inches wide, was certainly less securely fitted than the rest, it moved slightly when pushed. It would make a convenient weapon as he had no other. If at any time one man was so ill-advised as to come down alone, not being covered from the top by his friend with gun, something might be done. The rickety chair was of no use at all, it was far too light.

He sat down again and felt in his pockets, they had left him his cigarettes and he lit one. Better wait awhile in case they came back for the tray, though such courtesy was not to be expected. It happened, however, the trap overhead opened and the same two faces looked in. One of them said that they had a cup of coffee for him and something to read, and could he hand up the tray?

He did, and received a large cup of coffee in exchange and a bundle of illustrated papers. He thought this a good moment to protest about the electric light being turned off, and did so. They had undertaken, he said indignantly, to treat him with consideration. Could that be honestly said to include leaving him in semi-darkness? Besides, the lamp smelt.

"We regret," said Toto the Giraffe, who had to be the spokesman since the other man seldom uttered. "It is connected with the bolt. When the bolt is shot to keep the trap down, the light goes out. If we were electricians —but we are not. It would be insulting m'sieu's initiative to leave the trap unfastened, would it not?"

Hambledon said that though he regretted their refusal they had certainly worded it with the utmost delicacy. The men at the top looked at him with approval and said that it was well, he was being reasonable. If there was any other trifle he wanted it should be obtained. Hambledon said that he would like some more cigarettes before long and another box of matches; the men nodded and said they should come down with the evening meal. They then shut the flag-stone and Hambledon was left with the prospect of being undisturbed for some time. He drank his coffee with satisfaction; if the cellar was not damp it was horribly chilly.

A weapon might not be necessary. If one man came alone and handed him down a tray, the simplest method would be to reach up for it and seize the man's wrist instead. His position, lying on the floor with head, arms and shoulders over the edge, must be precarious unless he had his feet hooked round something, which was unlikely. An unexpected and violent tug should produce its effect and, if one dodged out of the way, contact with the stone floor would do the rest. Then there would be only one to deal with upstairs and on level terms; he might even be absent from the house. Tommy lit another cigarette, wrapped his legs in a blanket and cheered up. Those magazines might help to pass the time. He unrolled the bundle, which had been tied round with string, and then understood the sardonic amusement upon his jailers' faces, for the magazines were evidently Leonie's and of the Beautiful Woman type. Much about dress, much about beauty culture, a little about household management and the care of children, but mainly stories of the boy-meets-girl genre with consciously glamorous illustrations. Hambledon hurled them from him, growling, and looked about for other entertainment; once more the slightly loose piece of timber caught his eye.

They had taken away his knife and he had no coin large enough to use as a lever. He examined the bed and found a sort of swinging catch intended to hold the mattress in line with the frame, a piece of strip metal some two inches long loosely riveted at one end. He wrenched it off and began operations on the length of timber. It came forward a little, first at one end, then at the other; finally, with a scatter of small pieces of loose cement, it came out in his hands. He was pleased with it, it would serve well as a club. He put his piece of wood back into the wall, it was impossible to tell when the trapdoor above him might suddenly open. He flapped with his handkerchief at a tell-tale cascade of dust clinging to the wall below the hiding-place and finally picked up the rug on the floor wherewith to sweep the rest of the debris under the bed. When the rug was relaid there was no obvious sign of any disturbance.

When his jailers came with his supper they greeted him civilly, saying that they hoped the food was to his liking and that the cigarettes for which he had asked were on the tray. They lowered it down and Hambledon unbent sufficiently to thank them.

"Courage," added Toto. "It is not for much longer, probably. The negotiations of which I spoke, they are well begun." He had had a telephone conversation with someone in Paris who had told him that the laundress' white cat had been duly advertised in the *France-Soir*. "If you should wish for another blanket it shall be brought."

Hambledon said he would like another and one man went to fetch it while the other remained standing by the entrance. One man alone for a moment, but there seemed no chance of getting at him.

Toto returned. "Here is the blanket and also some papers perhaps more agreeable to your tastes."

"You are very amiable," said Tommy coldly, "all of a sudden."

"We wish no ill feelings," said the man seriously. "When this is all over you will say that you were well treated, will you not?"

Hambledon did not answer, after waiting a few

moments they wished him goodnight and closed the
slab. There followed the sound of the closing bolt and
again the electric light went out. The arrangement had
this advantage that they could not come upon him un-
awares, unless he was very sound asleep indeed the light
would warn him when the trap was about to be opened.

"Though I don't really see what good that does me,
unless I start digging a tunnel in the best tradition of
prison-breakers. It might come to that if they keep me
here long enough. One could use a piece of bedstead as a
trowel, I suppose I should emerge among the cabbages.
I wish I'd thought of asking for a pair of pyjamas,
probably there are some of Maurice's."

· · · · ·

When Alexandre Maurice walked out of the prison he
knew that he must leave Paris at once and for that it was
first necessary to get some money. He walked fast through
the streets, not a very safe proceeding since it could not
be long before all the police in Paris were looking for
him, but there was no alternative, he had not even the
few sous necessary for the tram fare. There were a few
people who would lend him money—not Colette, of
course, never more Colette—and he must have some
papers too. His Pierre Guyon papers would do, the police
knew nothing against that name. Better to go back to his
own room, the same from which the gang had dragged
him the night before. Some of them might be there,
going through his possessions; or the police, if they had
found out where he lived. No matter, he must be careful
in approaching it, that was all. There was money there,
and the papers too.

He made his way across Paris by lanes and alleys and passages, sometimes walking through shops with a second entrance in another street to avoid cross-roads where a policeman stood directing the traffic, and came at last to a tall old house, once the wing of a noble town residence but now leaning drunkenly between warehouses as being too decrepit to stand alone. Maurice came to it by way of the cellars, starting from a cobbler's shop at the bottom of a slimy stone stair down which the wines of Touraine and Anjou had been carried two hundred years earlier. There was still a square stone shelf with a niche above it for a lamp, the cobbler keeps his tools on it today but the wine-steward of the early seventeen-hundreds knew it well, he used it as a desk when he entered up his cellar-books.

Maurice nodded to the cobbler and passed on through a door at the back of the shop. Behind this door were long stone-flagged passages, shadowy and echoing at midday, impenetrably dark at night. He passed the great wine-cellars, now subdivided into airless rooms by panelling torn from the walls upstairs or rough planks stolen from some builder's yard, or even curtained off with rags and sacking, for people lived and died in these underground dens and the air was full of furtive noises and whispering. Maurice knew why, he was wearing sound shoes which gave out a firm tread, sound shoes are not worn by such as live there, he might be police. He saw no one at all but felt himself watched, a child began to cry and was abruptly hushed. Maurice shivered and hurried on. The passage turned, branched and turned again, the rooms here were smaller and more numerous, they were once the menservants' bedrooms. Their present inhabitants were a cut above the tenants of the wine-cellars, for these rooms had doors that would shut and even windows of a sort, so the air was fresher here, or at least a degree less mephitic.

He passed the foot of several flights of narrow stairs winding upwards, he knew that most of them had been bricked up at the top. There was another at the end of the last passage, he ran quietly up it and listened before he opened the door at the top. He heard one voice mumbling on alone; he nodded to himself, opened the door and entered a small room shabby and grimy enough but cheerfulness itself compared with those he had just passed. A small fire was burning in the grate and there was a coffee-pot on the hob; in an armchair by the fire an old woman was sitting reading the Bible aloud to herself. A pleasant picture until one heard what she was reading—

"*Asshur is there and all her company; his graves are about him: all of them slain, fallen by the sword;*

"*Whose graves are set in the sides of the pit, and her company is round about her grave: all of them slain, fallen by the sword which caused terror in the land of the living.*

"*There is Elam and all her multitude round about her grave, all of them slain, fallen by the sword——*"

"Who has died now?" broke in Maurice.

She looked up at him, one eye dark and bright and the other white with cataract.

"What? You frighten me, creeping in like that."

"You always read that dismal stuff," said Maurice, "and when anyone's died you read about graves. Who is it this time?" He sat on the edge of the table and lit a cigarette with an air of unconcern, but his fingers were not quite steady.

"Who's dead?" repeated the old woman. "Don't you know? You know, don't you? I knew you were coming this morning. I always know who's coming to see me, so I found the place ready for you. All of them slain, fallen by the sword. Only it wasn't a sword this time, was it? What did you do to her?"

"Who? I haven't done anything, only got into a bit of trouble with the police. Have they been here?"

"No. No, the police don't come here, why should they? They don't poke their noses in places like this. They don't even come and ask me to tell their fortunes. Maybe they think better not, eh?"

"So my room hasn't been entered?"

"I wouldn't say that," said the old woman thoughtfully, and Maurice started forward.

"Who's been here? Toto? Or the Rat-killer? Are they here now?" He edged towards the cellar stair.

"No, no. None of those men. No men at all, police or the other sort. Your room is all ready for you, you can go up in all confidence." She began to cackle with laughter and Maurice's spine crept.

"Who is up there?"

"You are such a fool, an imbecile, you do not even know what you have done. Listen. Everyone born is born with enough energy, animation, power, call it what you will, to last them for the length of life they were intended to have. Understand? If they are killed before that there is the unused energy still with them. Understand? So, when people are killed too soon, they do not stay dead. They cannot really go, perhaps their place is not ready for them——"

"I don't know what you're talking about——"

"Oh, I think you do. What was her name, that dark-haired woman you used to know? Colette, I think it was Colette, was it not——"

"You are mad," shrieked Maurice, "you always were mad and you're getting madder. They will take you away soon and lock you up——"

"Don't shout at me," she snapped, "I don't like it."

"I don't care what you like. Think you can frighten me with ghost stories? I didn't shoot Colette, Burenne did that——"

He broke off because she was looking interestedly over his shoulder, he tried to glance round but his muscles would not obey him.

"She says not," said the old woman in a suddenly cheerful voice. "She shakes her head and laughs and points at you. She ought to know, yes?"

Maurice tore his fingers from their convulsive grip of the table and rushed out of the further door, slamming it after him, but not before he had heard the monotonous voice beginning again. "*All of them slain, fallen*——"

He ran violently up the three flights of stairs to his own room, careless of who saw him though as chance would have it he met no one. Once inside the room he locked the door and set a chair under the handle as an extra safeguard before collapsing on the bed. That awful old woman, how would she know unless Colette had——

Nonsense. Colette was dead, he could still see the look of surprise in her face as he levelled the gun at her, and all this talk about the untimely dead not staying dead——

Of course. Obvious. Toto the Giraffe had been there at the flat with him. Unwise, of course, but he could not have managed alone. Someone had to bring Burenne to the door five minutes after he himself had entered, push him through the doorway and then fall flat when the shooting started. One shot for Burenne with Colette's gun, then one shot for Colette with Burenne's gun, drop them both in the right places and get away down the fire-escape. Toto's long neck bending round corners like an elephant's trunk with his head on the end of it, comic, that. Toto should have gone on the stage. Of course, Toto came here last night, after Maurice's arrest, to look for pickings. He told the old woman——

Maurice paused, for if there was one thing Toto was good at, it was holding his tongue. However, that's how it must have been. Toto told her and she put on that act to frighten him. Huh! Someone ought to wring her neck, probably somebody would one of these days.

It occurred to him suddenly to wonder whether Toto had found any pickings. He raised one floor-board which was screwed down, not nailed, but all was well. The money was there and so were his papers, he pocketed both. Now it was only to wait until nightfall and then get away, over the frontier into Belgium.

XIV

LEONIE

MAURICE crossed the Belgian frontier without troubling the frontier officials. He had an urgent errand to the bungalow at Laeken but he did not expect any difficulty in the matter because he thought the bungalow was empty, Leonie was in Paris. He wanted to find the German identity papers which he had used when he was working for the Van Hartmann concern in Milan. Leonie had them, they were the goad with which she drove him, they were the proof that he had not been a mysterious hero of the Resistance as he loved to hin but a full-blown collaborator with the Germans. He sat hunched up in the corner of a third-class railway carriage on his way to Brussels and his mouth twisted with loathing when he thought about Leonie. They made their way back from Northern Italy together after the German surrender; he looked back on that journey and thought what a fool he had been. Leonie had a perfectly good Belgian identity; at least, it was quite good enough to stand up to any ordinary investigation. She was going back to Brussels to take it up, she told him all about it during the interminable train journey. She was quite friendly and frank; as for him, he was bubbling over with happiness. The long nightmare was over, he was going back to Paris where he belonged, he would marry Colette and settle down to an honest job—well, approximately honest. Antique dealing, probably, he had learned a lot about antiques in Milan. He told Leonie his plans and she laughed and sympathised.

"At least you will hear no more from Goering about those alleged Monets," she said.

"He has other matters upon his mind now," agreed Maurice. "I shall be more careful in future. You know, I am beginning to think that in this business it might pay to be honest. What do you think?"

They parted in Paris upon quite friendly terms, Leonie went on to Brussels and Maurice rushed off to Colette. He would get a business post, as soon as ever he was settled they would get married, and Colette agreed.

"I am not," said Maurice magnificently, "the man to sponge upon my wife's earnings. No."

"No, no," said Colette earnestly. "You have had a hard and dangerous life in the Resistance, I am sure you have learned by now what is truly precious in life and what is but dross."

He nodded and promised amendment, but he remembered even then wishing that Colette would not preach. If only, even now, she would stop preaching—she had stopped. He had stopped her.

He shifted uneasily in his seat and looked unseeingly out of the window. Well, she had talked to the police so she deserved what she got. She had asked for it, going out to dinner with that Englishman who was hand-in-glove with the Sûreté. Carrying his carnations. They were in a vase in her flat the next evening, the place was scented with them. He shook the thought from him and returned to Leonie.

Work was not easy to get in Paris just after the liberation, there was confusion everywhere and continual movement of people going from Paris to where they belonged and returning to Paris from various forms of exile. Maurice was not the type who labours, he drifted naturally into the Black Market and throve on the shortage of stocks. Sometimes supplies were difficult to get and drastic measures had to be used. On one such occasion it had been necessary to raid a tobacconist's shop.

The raid went off perfectly and no one was even damaged. Maurice and his friends were happily engaged in sorting out the loot when a message was brought to him that a lady wanted to speak to him. Maurice scowled; if Colette had found out what he was really doing and had come after him with a sermon there would be trouble.

He went into another room and found there not Colette but a fluffy-haired blonde, much made up in a foolish exaggerated manner. It was a moment or two before he recognized her.

"Hilde! Why—what have you done to your hair?"

"Never mind my hair, and my name is Leonie now. Leonie Vermaas. How stupid you are, I told you that before we parted."

Maurice apologized; so much had happened since and the intervening months had been so busy——

"You mean that you expected never to see me again. You were mistaken, my dear Maurice. It is Maurice, your name, is it not?"

He said indignantly that it certainly was, it was his own real name in which he was born.

"Magnificent," said Leonie coolly. "No doubt you are now determined to bear it unsullied to the grave, are you not? Well, so you shall provided you do a little business for me. You need not draw back like that, I will pay you for it."

But Maurice continued to draw back. He did not know what Hilde—now Leonie—wanted with him but he was quite sure he wanted no more to do with her. That cold Teutonic efficiency should be exercised upon him no more if he could help it. Leonie took no notice of his protests. She told him that it was a simple matter, just putting a few notes into circulation here and there as he was so well able to do with his present business connections.

Maurice said bluntly that he would first burn the damned things.

"Oh no," said Leonie. "That would be most unwise."

"It is you who are unwise," said Maurice angrily. "Unless you go away and cease to pester me I shall inform the police exactly who you are."

"You have proofs?" said Leonie sweetly. "No? How very unfortunate. Because, you see, two can play at that game and I have got proofs. Your German identity papers, you know. Complete with photograph. You remember, don't you? No, it is no use calling me rude names. You wouldn't like your friends to know you were a collaborator, would you? Let alone the police?"

Maurice still refused so she nodded at him and went away. The next morning the police arrested him for the tobacco raid; when he came up for trial he looked towards the public benches to see if Colette were there. She was, her face drawn and full of pity; two rows behind her he saw Leonie laughing at him. He was convicted and served his sentence.

Maurice gave in after that, he saw no alternative.

One task led to another; in a few months' time he was as firmly shackled as ever he had been in Milan when Leonie had only to give the order for him to be shot. He would have delighted to murder her but that he understood she had arranged, in the event of her death, for the papers to be made public. "So you had better do your utmost to keep me alive, hadn't you?"

He did discover that the papers were somewhere at the bungalow though so long as Leonie was there he had never been able to search the place. Now, at last, she was in Paris and he on his way to Laeken. The place should be taken to pieces but he would find the papers. If not, the house should burn with everything in it. This was the end——

The train pulled into the Midi station at Brussels and drew to a stop.

Maurice spent the early part of the evening in a cinema and went out to Laeken after nightfall. He approached the bungalow with extreme caution across the market gardens at the back and scouted round the house under cover of bushes. There was someone in the house, there were lights in two of the rooms.

He almost abandoned his project then and there. After all, if he could travel from Paris to Laeken in the time so could Leonie; much more quickly, in fact, if she came on the *Etoile du Nord* or the *Oiseau Bleu* expresses. There was just a chance that the person in the house was a local woman whom Leonie employed as a cleaner. He knew that Leonie did leave this woman a key to the house if it were to be empty for more than two or three days so that she could get in to air the place and tidy up. She was scrupulously honest and all dangerous secrets were securely locked up. He decided to wait awhile, perhaps she would go away.

Maurice heard voices in the road; stationary voices, not passing talkers, just by the gate; he peered through a screen of lilac and saw by the light of a street lamp two workmen in a patch of road which was cordoned off. They were very leisurely engaged in taking up the road, encouraged by two friends who leaned on bicycles and watched them.

Presently there came a sound from the house, the front door opened and a man came out. He was silhouetted for a moment against the lighted hall as he turned to call back an answer to someone else inside. "All right," he said. "I'll not forget them," and both outline and voice were, Maurice thought, familiar. The man walked down the path and received illumination from the lights of a passing car, it was one of Leonie's gang, the man called The Rat-killer.

Maurice stood perfectly still against a tree and the man did not see him but walked unconcernedly through the gate and along the road towards Brussels. "Going out for a drink," said Maurice to himself. "One less in the house, who else is there?"

The two loiterers with the bicycles broke off their conversation with the workmen, mounted their machines and rode slowly away in the direction taken by The Rat-killer; the workmen resumed their unhurried labours and Maurice made his way to the house. If there was only one other in the house now was his chance, he could deal with one alone always provided it was not Leonie. He crept round from one window to another and was rewarded by the sight of Toto the Giraffe in the kitchen peeling potatoes. There seemed to be no one else.

Maurice entered by the front door since it had been left unlocked for the return of The Rat-killer and there was no one about to see him except, of course, the road-diggers who did not count. He slipped the catch as he entered in order that he should not be disturbed, and walked quietly down the passage into the kitchen. Toto, who had finished peeling and was now slicing, looked up from his potatoes and saw Maurice standing by the door.

"Maurice!"

"That's me," said Maurice, and took a step forward.

"You are mad to come here," said Toto, and flung the potato knife straight at him. Maurice, however, was expecting this and swung aside, the knife passed his arm and stuck in the panel of the door and immediately the battle was joined French apache fashion, kicking included and no holds barred. Hambledon in the cellar below heard even through stone flags the sound of combat overhead, particularly when a pot containing soup fell off the stove and rolled upon the floor.

In the meantime the road-diggers outside, who were much more interested in events at the bungalow than Maurice realized, saw the light from the hall when the front door was opened and the outline of a man going in. They stopped work at once, and rightly, since they were not Corporation employees at all but plain-clothed police who had been given the task of watching the bungalow at the request of Letord. Not that he really expected much help from it in the search for Hambledon, but there was no trace of him in Paris and the bungalow was under suspicion, naturally. It was just a chance which ought not to be neglected. When the Belgian police reported that there were two men there and the descriptions applied to Toto the Giraffe and The Rat-killer, Letord asked that they should be closely watched but not molested unless either or both of them left the house. If they did, could they please be arrested at once. He, Letord, was starting for Brussels immediately by air.

The two policemen accordingly set down their picks and looked at each other.

"That one, who was he and where did he come from?"

"Across the garden, evidently. Impossible to recognize at this range. We should go up to the house and try to see what is happening?"

"Or wait for the other two to return with their prisoner? If we alarm the men at the house, we might not be able to prevent their escape."

"That is so. Our men will not be long—in fact, here they come."

Three figures approached along the road in the light of the street lamps, the two outside were the policemen with bicycles who had been idling while the others un-hurriedly dug and the man in the middle was The Rat-killer, securely handcuffed. When they all met a short conference was held, after which The Rat-killer found himself with the links of his handcuffs round a tree in the garden while the four policemen went up to the house.

By that time the kitchen light was out, but through a gap in the curtains of Leonie's bedroom Maurice could be seen energetically hunting for something. He was pulling the drawers right out of the dressing-table and feeling about in the spaces where they had been, measuring the depth for a concealed space behind. He had already dragged up the carpet for signs of a moveable floor-board. While they watched he abandoned the dressing-table to attack the chest of drawers.

"That is Alexandre Maurice, the prisoner who escaped from here before," said one of the policemen in a whisper. "Giraud, to the front of the house. Emil, to the back. Henri, with me. I am going in through this window."

He waited till his men had time to take up position, smashed the glass with the butt of his revolver and proceeded to scramble in. At the first crash Maurice leaped for the bedroom door and shut it after him, there came the sound of a key turning in the lock.

It did not take the police long to get in and they searched the bungalow thoroughly. They knew that Maurice had not come out, but look where they would they could not find him. They found Toto the Giraffe unconscious in a pool of soup upon the kitchen floor; him they handcuffed to avoid mischance, but of Maurice there was no sign. Eventually and very unwillingly they rang up police headquarters and told their unsatisfactory story. They received no sympathy and a police sergeant came out to them at once, the same man who had arrested Hambledon at the house in the Rue Olive. He heard their story and then examined the premises for himself, including the space under the roof.

"He does not appear to be here," admitted the sergeant. "You are completely satisfied that he did not escape from the house at the outset?"

The four policemen explained their reasons for being sure that he had not and the sergeant nodded.

"Then he is still within."

He sat down upon a chair in the kitchen and disregarded formality sufficiently to light a cigarette. He sat there, letting his eyes wander round the room and observing carefully every detail he saw; the constable called Giraud stood before him in the attitude of a dog hoping that someone will throw a stick, the other three were on guard outside the house.

The sergeant's eyes fell upon two electric-light switches beside the door, he looked from them to the one light in the ceiling. The switches were of the kind which are turned round, not up or down.

"Why are there two switches and only one light?" he asked, and went to try them.

"Perhaps there was a second light here which has been took away," suggested Giraud.

The upper switch operated the ceiling light, the other produced no visible effect. The sergeant began to say that no doubt that was the explanation but Giraud put his head on one side and said: "Do that again."

The sergeant turned the switch twice.

"It makes a small noise somewhere," said Giraud. "Somewhere over here, by the stove. A noise like 'plonk'."

"It may be the master switch for the stove," said the sergeant. "Switch on the griller and see if it works."

The griller bars glowed red and were unaffected whether the switch by the door were on or off.

"It's not that," said the sergeant. "I expect you were right, it is some light which is now disused."

"Then why does something move?"

"Come over here," said the sergeant, "and work the switch while I listen."

XV

SOLDIER OF THE LEGION

MAURICE dashed out of the bedroom as the window-pane broke, locked the door behind him and ran along the passage towards the garden door. Before he reached it he heard someone there trying to get in so he turned into the kitchen, slid across the soup-greased floor to the electric stove and tried to push it over. It would not lift; of course not, it was kept bolted in order to switch off the cellar light. He rushed back to the switches by the door and turned the lower one. There was another crash in the house behind him, the police had broken in somewhere else.

Frantic with haste, he tilted back the stove, holding the edge of the trap with his hand and stepped down upon the first rung of the ladder. His shoes were greasy and would not hold him, he slithered down to the floor and the trap slammed shut over his head. He had turned in falling and seen that there was someone already there; even as he staggered to regain his balance his gun was already in his hand.

"I say," said Hambledon admiringly, "you are quick on the draw, aren't you?"

"Drop that club!"

Hambledon dropped it at once, there is no arguing with a revolver pointed at your chest. "I may say that if I'd known it was you doing the Demon King act in reverse I'd have clouted you before your feet touched the ground."

"Why did you not?"

"You might possibly have been a friend of mine."

"Let me advise m'sieu'," said Maurice impudently, "to hit first and identify afterwards, in future."

"Police after you?" asked Hambledon casually. "Or Toto and supporting company?"

"What business is that of yours?"

"Not a bit matey, are you? Who threw the cooking-pot just now? Didn't it remind you of something? It did me."

Maurice did not answer for a moment, he appeared to be thinking. There was no sound from overhead, the police were elsewhere in the house. When he spoke again it was in a slightly more conciliatory tone.

"This Toto. You have seen him here?"

"Yes," said Hambledon, surprised. "Quite recently, about an hour ago. Of course he may have gone away again, my view of the outside world——"

"Have the goodness to tell me when he came here, if you know." Hambledon hesitated, and Maurice added: "It is a small private matter only, it cannot possibly concern you in any degree."

"We came from Paris here together, in the same car they were trying to get you into."

Maurice frowned. "This was—when? The same evening?"

"The same moment. We drove instantly away."

"But Toto. He went into a house near there, if only for a few minutes, yes?" Hambledon shook his head. "Or he spoke to an old woman blind of one eye?"

"He spoke to no one and we drove away at once. Be

reasonable. The street was full of people yelling 'Assassins! Police!' Would they linger?"

Maurice relapsed into silence. Only he and Toto knew how Colette died; if Toto had not told the old woman—— His expression became so absent that Hambledon braced himself for a spring, but heavy footsteps sounded overhead and Maurice returned to the present.

"Don't speak!" he whispered. "If you do, I'll shoot you dead."

"Then they'll hear that," Hambledon whispered back, "and you won't be any better off."

"That won't help you," hissed Maurice—since they were speaking French the phrase lent itself to hissing—and he cocked his head to listen. It did not take the police overhead long to search the kitchen and handcuff Toto, after which there was silence and a long pause while they were waiting for the arrival of the sergeant from Brussels.

"They appear to be brooding," said Hambledon. "Or do you think they've gone?"

"We will wait for some time before we move," said Maurice, resting his right hand in the crook of his left elbow. "This gun, it becomes heavy," he added, by way of explanation. "Tell me, if the police do go, taking with them Toto and the Rat-killer, you will be sensible, will you not?"

"What course of action," said Hambledon cautiously, "would you regard as sensible?"

"That I go my way and you go yours. What? You are not a Belgian policeman or a French one either and why do their work? Me, I have no taste for murder, why should I kill you?"

"It does sound sensible," said Tommy, who did not

believe a word of it and was a little annoyed that Maurice should think him green enough to agree. "As for murder, that is your affair, is it not?"

"What the devil d'you mean—murder is my affair?"

"Since you are armed and I am not," explained Hambledon.

"Oh, ah. Yes. It is logical, that."

Heavy footsteps passed overhead and Hambledon remarked that the gentlemen were still in possession. Another silence followed during which his mind ran, as it so often did, upon the murder of Colette. He decided to try a little fishing expedition and began by offering Maurice his condolences. "On the loss of a gracious friend. I refer, of course, to Mademoiselle Colette Masurel. I had the pleasure of meeting her again in Paris. A tragic loss."

Maurice's eyes narrowed. "Thank you. A great loss, as you say."

"So cruel," said Hambledon, "so pointless. I gather that you had known each other from childhood."

"She——" Maurice swallowed and began again. "She talked about me, then?"

"A little, about your early days. There was a story about a kitten of hers which you rescued from a tall tree and another about an old man who sold chestnuts. I gather that she rescued you that time."

Maurice barely smiled. "I remember, yes. Ah, these early days!" he added perfunctorily.

Hambledon tried a cast in another direction. "There is one thing I should like to tell you," he said earnestly. "It was evident to me that she knew nothing of your present way of living and, believe me, I did not tell her."

Maurice turned perfectly white and the gun drooped in his hand, Hambledon watched it like a cat watching a mouse and went on talking. "Not out of regard for your feelings at all, it was just that I did not want to hurt her. For women of that type there is enough suffering in this life without——"

Maurice broke in. "She told you nothing about me—since our childhood? But she told the police——"

"Nothing. She was anxious about you, yes, because you had once been convicted, but that was in the records. I know, I was there when she was interrogated."

"It's working," Hambledon said to himself, "it's working," for Maurice's face was like that of a man in hell. "He did think she betrayed him and he shot her himself. If only he'll shut his eyes or burst into tears——"

He could have stamped with anger when footsteps overhead once more broke the spell and the moment passed. Maurice recovered himself and the gun was level and steady again. A few minutes later they were both startled when the light went out and on again at once.

"I missed a chance there. If they do it again——"

Minutes passed while the sergeant in the kitchen above them puzzled over the uses of the second switch. When the light did go out again Hambledon was ready, he sprang at Maurice, knocked his gun up with one hand and hit him under the jaw with the other. He was fortunate with the gun for Maurice dropped it, but the blow did not knock him out and the fight started. Hambledon jumped back to avoid a savage kick, crashed into the chair and knocked the oil lamp off it on to the bed where it upset, pouring paraffin over the blankets, and burst into flames which leaped nearly to the ceiling and began to run along

the floor. The electric light went on and off almost un-
noticed while Hambledon recoiled from the flames and
Maurice tried to smother the fire by dragging up the rug.
The room filled with choking black smoke and Hambledon, blinded and coughing, shouted at the top of his
voice for help, help! "Open the trap!"

Smoke began to drift into the kitchen round the edges
of the trap-door and told the sergeant what he wished to
know. He turned the switch once more, Maurice rushed
up the ladder and pushed open the trap closely followed
by Hambledon and a column of black smoke such as
occurs when one burns paraffin-soaked blankets. Maurice
was immediately knocked down, knelt upon and handcuffed; Hambledon would have received the same greet-
ing but that the sergeant recognized his voice and general
appearance, his face was blackened with smoke and his
coat was smouldering.

The sergeant patted out the sparks and said that he
had been instructed to find M. Hambledon and that he
was glad to have succeeded. "The fire, is it serious?"

Hambledon, choking and mopping his streaming eyes,
said he thought that most of the paraffin had by now been
consumed and that a few buckets of water would extinguish the blankets. The sergeant called in his other
constables and set them to it while Tommy retired to the
bathroom, Leonie's luxurious Coty bath-soap and comparatively untainted air. He was still enjoying himself
when Letord came in expecting to find Toto the Giraffe
and The Rat-killer under arrest. He had been told of their
capture while he was being driven from Brussels airport,
but at the sight of Hambledon alive and unhurt he was
almost lyrical. When the sergeant came from the kitchen

and said that they had Maurice also, Letord became businesslike at once.

"He was looking for something, that one," said the sergeant, and described how he had seen through the window Maurice frantically searching Leonie's bedroom.

"He did not, apparently, find it? No, I see. What is this stench of paraffin?"

Hambledon explained.

"And where is Maurice?" asked Letord. "In the kitchen. I think he would be better in jail, do you not agree? The other two, also, yes. Where are they? In separate rooms, how sensible of you."

The sergeant said that he was expecting the police van at any moment and Letord said that he wondered what Maurice was looking for but as it would not be the slightest use asking him he did not propose to waste breath in doing so.

"Hunting through Leonie's things," said Tommy thoughtfully. "I also wonder what for, since he must have known the police would search the place after he was first arrested. Did you," he asked the Belgian sergeant, "find anything interesting here when you searched?"

"Except for the false money in vast quantities, no, m'sieu'."

"I do not understand why he should search the woman's things," said Letord. "I cannot imagine he would take such an one deeply into his confidence."

"I forgot you didn't know," said Hambledon. "She's up to the neck in it. She drove the car when they tried to abduct Maurice and got me instead. She gave the orders all through that performance and the others jumped to it. She gave me the hypodermic when I was drugged, with the other two holding me down. I didn't see her again after that, I don't know where she is now."

"So she was in Paris," said the sergeant. "It was understood here that she went to Roubaix."

"Oh, no doubt she did," said Tommy. "She just didn't stay there."

"I have made a mistake," said Letord mournfully. "I did not realize the importance of that woman. Moreover, it is odd, is it not? She tries to abduct Maurice and he resists violently, calling for help. Yet he comes here alone. This thing, whatever it is, he must want it very badly."

The police van came, removed the prisoners and went away again; Hambledon, Letord and the Belgian sergeant walked round the deserted house looking rather hopelessly about them. They ended in the kitchen, having found nothing for which it was possible to imagine Maurice risking his life and liberty. Letord looked idly at a calendar hanging on the wall, a small gay picture of the modern French school set in a thick cardboard mount with the last sheet of dates still stuck upon the lower edge; December 1945, the others having been torn off.

"Odd how people keep out-of-date calendars," he remarked.

"I expect she liked the picture," said Hambledon, looking at it over his shoulder. "It is nice, it's charming. Expensively got up, too, the mount is nearly half an inch thick."

"Must have cost a lot," said Letord, turning away. "A present from some fool, I expect. Well, sergeant?"

"It is an impediment to efficient search," said the sergeant gloomily, "not to have the faintest idea of what it is for which one looks."

"It is axiomatic," said Letord.

"Formidable," said Hambledon.

They returned to Brussels, leaving one constable to guard the bungalow, and proceeded at once to the interrogation of the prisoners. The man called The Ratkiller gave them no help at all, merely replying in answer to all questions either that he didn't know or that he wasn't there or both. He seemed neither sullen nor frightened nor even interested; he looked at them occasionally out of dull eyes but most of the time he merely stared vaguely at the floor. As each question was put to him he took a moment to consider it but the replies were always the same, either "*Sais pas*" or "*N'etais pas là.*" Eventually Letord gave him up in disgust, the Belgian Superintendent shrugged his shoulders and both glanced at Hambledon.

"One question," said Tommy. "Listen, prisoner. Did you know a woman called Colette Masurel?"

"No."

"You are quite sure? She is dead now."

"Never heard of her."

Hambledon sat back in his chair and the Belgian ordered this man to be removed and Toto the Giraffe to be brought in instead. While they were waiting Letord said that evidently Hambledon was still exercising his mind upon that closed case. "Behold your English bulldog," he said to the Belgian. "Here you see him in the act of not letting go."

Hambledon merely smiled and Toto was brought in. He was a very different type; more talkative, more intelligent and much more nervous. The Belgian, after a few preliminary questions, handed him over to Letord who hitched up his chair and set about him. In ten minutes The Giraffe had contradicted himself four times and given three mutually exclusive accounts of why Hambledon was imprisoned in the cellar.

"Miserable vermin," cried Letord, thumping the table. "The truth, if you know what that is! I will have the truth out of you if I have to sit here asking you questions until midday next Sunday. Now then! You fetched Maurice out of that rabbit-warren where he lived in Paris. You cannot deny that, this gentleman saw you. Who told you to do that?"

"I—I don't know."

"Man or woman?"

"I don't know."

"You mean the person was so disguised that you did not know whether it was a man or a woman?"

Toto wriggled in his chair and his long neck swayed from side to side, for some reason the sinuous motion made Hambledon feel sick.

"Answer me! Man or woman?"

"Man," said Toto, and glanced up to see if they believed him.

"Describe him."

"Can't. Never saw him."

"Never saw him, eh? What was his name?"

"I don't know. You see, I didn't know him, that's what I meant just now when I said I didn't know whether it was a man or a woman. I suppose it was a man but it might have been a woman, I don't know. He—or she, if you insist—used to send messages or write notes." Toto was plainly gaining confidence.

"I don't believe one word of this," murmured Hambledon to Letord.

"Nor I. Prisoner! Who drove the car on that occasion?"

"Somebody I didn't know. It was dark, I——"

"Careful," said Hambledon. "I was there, you know."

"Then why ask me?" said Toto.

"Because," thundered Letord, "you are charged with kidnapping, aggravated assault, unlawful administration of a noxious drug, illegal imprisonment—probably attempted murder——"

"No, no," broke in Toto. "Ask this gentleman, he will tell you that he was treated with the most distinguished consideration and——"

Letord made a rude noise.

"But it is true," persisted Toto. "I cooked his meals myself, I bought him cigarettes——"

"Anything to keep him quiet till you were ready to murder him. You know the penalty for all that, don't you? Transportation for life."

"M'sieu'," said Toto, addressing Hambledon. "I did my best for you, help me now!"

"Why should I," asked Hambledon, "when you won't help the police?"

Toto paused. "If I do my best to help you, it will be better for me, yes?"

"It will be a lot worse if you don't," said Letord grimly. "Now then. What do you know about the woman who drove the car?"

Toto knew very little, he had seen her for the first time two days before the kidnapping. "I was a friend of Maurice," he said. "I think he worked for her in Belgium. Then there was some sort of quarrel and Maurice went away. She told us that we take orders from her now, instead. I don't like her," he added in the accents of truth, "she frightens me." He described going to get

Maurice and rather unwillingly acquiring Hambledon instead. "We could not wait, he would not let go, so we took him. She told us to bring him here, she came with us to the frontier. Then she went back to Paris to get Maurice. This gentleman, he was for swops."

Letord nodded, they knew this to be true. "Now about Maurice. What's his game?"

"Passing 'slush', m'sieu'. He is a big noise in that racket." Toto spoke much more confidently, it was plain that Maurice inspired him with no such terror as did Leonie.

"How long have you know him?"

"Many years, many years. Since before the War. He was a dealer in pictures then, other things also but mainly pictures." Toto grinned. "He sold three to Goering, he told me, for thousands of francs, such nice pictures. Then some experts saw them and Goering wanted his money back. So Maurice left Paris."

"Where did he go?"

"He said he joined the Resistance, m'sieu'."

"He said so, don't you believe it?"

Toto shrugged his shoulders. "I do not know. I was deported for forced labour in Germany, I was away almost three years."

"Then why don't you believe it?"

"There was a man in a *bistro* one night, he came in by chance, you understand? He knew Maurice, he said, he had seen him in Milan. Maurice shut him up, but I do not think the French Resistance operated in Milan."

Letord asked about the organization for passing forged notes and Toto answered with the utmost frankness but it was immediately clear that he knew very little, his evidence was little more than a series of anecdotes of the few occasions when he had helped Maurice in some degree.

"You don't appear to be at all frightened of Maurice," remarked Hambledon, and Toto smiled. "What's the joke?"

Toto became confidential. "Messieurs. You did not promise to help me if I helped you, I understand that, it is not done. Nevertheless, I have helped you, have I not? If I help you yet further, will you permit that I join the Foreign Legion and go right away and not return for years? Look, you shall take me to Marseilles and you shall see me sign on for five years, I make a good soldier, I like soldiering. It is a bargain, yes?"

"You slimy piece of ullage," began Letord, but Toto only smiled.

"Something you very much want to know," he said ingratiatingly. "Why not? I have done nothing very bad and France wants soldiers, does she not? I tell you, I make a good soldier. It is for France, m'sieu'."

Letord's mouth twitched and Hambledon burst into laughter echoed by the deep "Ho—ho—ho" of the Belgian Superintendent of Police. "He has plenty of impertinence, that one," he said.

"Besides," added Toto, "there is this advantage for me also in the *Legion Etrangère*; Madame Leonie, she cannot follow me there."

"I should do a deal," said Hambledon in English.

"Very well," said Letord. "Doubtless you deserve the guillotine but we can always attend to that later. When you come out of the *Legion Etrangère*, for example."

Toto described in detail exactly how Maurice had murdered both Burenne and Colette Masurel.

XVI

THE CALENDAR

WHEN Toto the Giraffe had been withdrawn the three men round the table looked at each other.

"It is true, you know," said Hambledon. "He described the scene as he could not have done unless he had been there, the attitudes of the bodies, the position of the guns, everything. Even the smell of carnations in the room."

Letord nodded. "He was there, certainly, and I do not think he did the murders himself. Why should he? We will see what Maurice has to say. In the meantime I take off my hat to the British bull-dog. I salute him with the deepest respect."

"I talked to Maurice about Colette while we were in the cellar," said Hambledon, and described the scene. "I was certain then that he had done it."

"He is a vicious animal, that type," said the Belgian. "She has comforted and helped him all his life, but at the first breath of suspicion does he remember that? No. He shoots her, snake that he is. He cannot trust, that is the way of it."

"I hope she haunts him," said Hambledon.

"Shall we have him in?" asked Letord. "Or—no, it is getting late and our English colleague should retire. He has had enough diversions these last few days, he should rest. If one might use your telephone, m'sieu', to ring up the Hotel Albert Premier, he would feel at home there."

"I will speak to them myself," said the Superintendent, and did so. "They have a room for you," he added at the end of the conversation, "the same you had before. They ask me to say that they are honoured."

"Thank you," began Hambledon, "your kindness——" but at that point the telephone rang again. The Superintendent took the call.

"A woman? You are sure?" He put his hand over the mouthpiece for a moment and interjected "At the bungalow" to Letord and Hambledon. "You are certain she did get inside? Yes. In the kitchen. What were you doing, having a nap? No idea what she did, I suppose? Well, she might have left a time-bomb, if so no doubt you will notice it in due course. Can you describe her? Slim, and ran like a young woman, that's a lot of help. Yes, I know it's dark, it generally is at midnight. Took what? What picture? Oh, the calendar in the kitchen, I remember it. Nothing else so far as——"

Hambledon sat up suddenly and banged the desk, the Superintendent said "Wait" to the telephone and "What is it?" to Hambledon who was muttering to himself.

"What Maurice was looking for," he said. "Papers of some kind, probably incriminating. To him or someone else. They were behind the picture, in the mount, I said it was too thick and I'll bet my last shilling that was Leonie."

"Ha," said the Superintendent. "You stay there," he said into the telephone, "I'll attend to you presently."

He replaced the receiver and turned to Hambledon. "You think———"

"She will get away," said Hambledon urgently.

"Not by train at this hour," said Letord, who seemed to carry the railway time-tables of Europe in his head. "In a hired car, possibly———"

"Or by air," said Tommy. "I should, in her place. You can hire planes by private charter from this airport, can't you?"

"Certainly," said the Superintendent. "We can check that at once." He telephoned to the airport and asked if anyone had chartered a plane to leave Brussels that night, now, within the hour. "Yes? Who? Madame Duval, I'm not interested in her name, what does she look like? Short, slim, fair-haired—listen. Has she arrived there yet? Listen. When she does, she is not to leave. Important, police orders. Good God, no, don't tell her that on any account. Make some excuse, engines want adjusting, anything. Be polite and casual, put her in the waiting-room and give her a drink. Car coming in now? Well, get on with it, I am coming at once."

The Superintendent, with Hambledon and Letord at his heels, bustled out of the office bellowing for a car at once and two constables.

"Do you think," said Hambledon in a low voice to Letord, "that he will drive us himself?"

"Without doubt," said Letord grimly.

But the Superintendent put his hand on the horn and kept it there and the traffic in the streets melted before his path. Only when they drew near the airport did their progress become quieter, they shot through the gates and came up to the office buildings to find the duty staff waiting for them on tiptoe. Out on the tarmac an engine was warming up and all the runway lights were on.

"She is in the lounge, messieurs, this way."

There were several doors to the lounge, the party split up to cover them all and then entered with a run. Leonie was sitting in an easy chair with a glass of wine beside her, she looked round and snatched up her handbag but Letord seized one arm and a constable the other.

"Mademoiselle Leonie Vermaas," said the Superintendent, removing the handbag out of her reach, "I arrest you on a charge of dealing in forged currency and I am taking you now to the police station where you will be formally charged. Handcuff her, men, one hand to each of you, and watch her closely, she may carry poison."

"How completely ridiculous," she said coldly. "What grounds have you for this absurd charge?"

"Plenty," said Letord. "We have Maurice."

It was as though he had struck her, she swayed and turned perfectly white, her features sharpened and her mouth became a thin line but she did not speak.

"The picture," said Letord, "where is it?"

"Perhaps she's sitting on it," said Hambledon.

She was pulled to her feet; behind her in the chair was a flat brief-case such as business-men use, Letord snatched it up.

"Why, it isn't even locked," he said gleefully, and pulled out the calendar. The back of the mount was not solid, even to the eye there was plainly only a border of card round a recess which had thin paper pasted over it. Letord's fingers twitched to rip it off but the Belgian Superintendent intervened.

"At the station, my friend, at the station. You can enjoy yourself better there."

"You will find there," said Leonie Vermaas, "some interesting information about Maurice."

"When he was in Milan, mademoiselle?" asked Hambledon blandly.

"You know that—already?"

"No doubt you can fill any little gaps in our knowledge, mademoiselle."

"Take her away," said the Superintendent; and watched her being led from the room.

"She must have had a shock, you know," said Hambledon, "when she walked into the bungalow and found a constable in possession. I suppose she just grabbed the calendar and ran."

"I will have full details of that business in the morning," said the Superintendent grimly. "Probably she saw him there and got in without being seen. He says he was patrolling round the house and saw her running away from it."

When the calendar was torn open at the police station the contents were most informative. There were the German identity papers which Maurice had carried at Milan, in them he was described as the confidential clerk to Herr Van Hartmann, antique dealer.

"Van Hartmann!" said Hambledon. "Now see the cats come leaping out of the bag. He was the German agent in Italy for the distribution of the notes printed at Sachsenhausen, a friend of mine helped to unravel him. He used to buy antiques with them—and Maurice was a picture-dealer, so he was. It all hangs together. The man Van Hartmann had a brace of alleged wives in different places, could Leonie have been one of them? It will be quite easy to find out, there are plenty of people who knew them."

"Perhaps Maurice could be persuaded to tell us," said the Belgian Superintendent. "What else have we? A neat little notebook bound in green leather containing a list of names and addresses. Let me see, some in my country and some in yours, my dear Letord. How businesslike is Leonie, what a hotel manageress was lost in her. What have you there?"

"Raw material for blackmail," said Letord. "This, no doubt, is how she persuaded these people to work for her. One gentleman has served a term of imprisonment for forgery under another name, both names and dates given. Is he in your list? Yes, I thought he might be. Most of them seem to have been collaborators like Maurice who want their pasts forgotten. Here's an informer. You will see to him, won't you? Ah, and here's a Gestapo agent now running a green-grocer's shop in Antwerp, he can kiss his cabbages goodbye I imagine——"

So it went on. What impressed Hambledon was the extraordinarily compact manner in which Leonie had filed her dossiers. Written with a fine pen upon sheets no thicker and not much larger than cigarette-papers, there was as much information as would occupy a fair-sized filing cabinet in so little bulk as could easily be held in one hand. They were cross-indexed and connected with the names in the notebook by a system as simple as it was effective.

"Hotel manageress indeed," he said. "She could manage the Army & Navy Stores. She'd better come over to England and reform the Civil Service."

"These papers," said the Superintendent, "must go to my superior officers. Action will follow at once."

"By the way," said Hambledon, "is Papa there? The old chap who kept that house in the Rue Olive. And his half-section the dock porter who wanted to shoot me, what was his name? Shaef, no, Schaer. You had them in custody, hadn't you? What happened?"

"Nothing, yet," said the Superintendent, turning over pages in the notebook. "Yes, they are here. We had to postpone their trial until Schaer was well enough to talk, he had his jaw broken in that fracas with the Jews, you remember. He is still in hospital but I think the case comes on next week. Or was to have done so, it all ties up with this now."

"They didn't shoot Yanni-the-Nephew, you know," said Tommy. "Burenne did, and he's dead so that's cleared up."

There came a tap at the door; the Superintendent covered the papers with a blotter before he called " Come in." A police-sergeant entered and reported that the prisoner Maurice had attempted to commit suicide by hanging in his cell but had been noticed by the warder and cut down. He was little the worse. "Physically, that is," added the sergeant. "I think his brain is going. He thinks there is a woman in his cell. You can see his eyes following her round. Uncanny, it is really."

"Indeed," said Hambledon, deeply interested. "Does he talk to her?"

"He has some difficulty in talking at the moment, m'sieu'. The throat, you know. One can but make out a name, it sounds like Colette." He left the room.

"You, m'sieu'," said Letord to Hambledon, "expressed a wish that she might haunt him. She seems to have heard you."

Hambledon shivered and said that if they would excuse him he would go to bed for what was left of the night. "You have broken open this mystery, gentlemen. Leonie was the head of it, I do not doubt. I suppose that after the Germans were finished she took it on again for Russia. You have put a stop to that."

"Until they find somebody else," said Letord gloomily. "Yes, go and rest, m'sieu', I will come and call upon you in the morning."

Hambledon walked across the Place Rogier, still brilliantly floodlit although the hour was past three o'clock in the morning, and there was still fast traffic to be dodged in crossing the Rue de Brabant. He entered the Hotel Albert and found the night porter expecting him.

"Let m'sieu' be welcome! The manager desired me to say what a pleasure it is to see m'sieu' return. He waited until half-an-hour ago to see m'sieu' himself, but——"

"I'm sorry he should have done that," said Hambledon, and yawned irrepressibly. "I was delayed but if I'd known I would have rung up."

"Speaking of ringing up," said the porter.

"What," said Hambledon feebly, "not——"

"Yes, m'sieu'. The same lady as when m'sieu' was here before, she gave the name of Brigitte. She said that she and her friend had seen you pass in a car with the police and she feared lest you had been arrested."

"If she rings again," said Hambledon, "tell her that all is well and that I will try to see her in the morning for a few minutes before I leave for England."

"Very good, m'sieu'."

"Do not put the call through to my room. I desire undisturbed sleep."

"It is understood, m'sieu'."

"Goodnight," said Hambledon, turning towards the lift, and at that moment the telephone bell rang.

Tommy Hambledon cast an agonized glance at the porter and ran like a hare.

For regular early information

about

FORTHCOMING NOVELS

send a postcard

giving your name and address

to

THE FICTION EDITOR
HODDER & STOUGHTON LTD.
3, St. Paul's House, Warwick Square,
London, E.C.4